A person could die
from getting as scared as this.

Lost. Temporarily, it had to be temporarily!

Where were those friends who promised they would take care of me in these horrible mountains? The friends who had talked me into this monster trip?

"People get lost in the Sierra every summer." The ominous words came back to me. "Some of them are never seen again." They had to come for me! Soon! Before the bears came back! A person could die from getting as scared as this.

And then I heard it. The most beautiful, piercing sound I had ever heard: a whistle. And someone calling, "Bennet, Bennet!" Phillip Hargrove had come back to find me.

I was so happy! I forgot totally that I had planned never to speak to him again.

**Other Apple Paperbacks
you will enjoy:**

JUST
← A LITTLE BIT →
LOST

Laurel Trivelpiece

AN
APPLE
PAPERBACK

SCHOLASTIC INC.
New York Toronto London Auckland Sydney

For My Trailmates

ISBN 0-590-41465-8

12 11 10 9 8 7 6 5 4 3 2 1   8 9/8 0 1 2 3/9

Printed in the U.S.A.   01

First Scholastic printing, March 1988

Chapter 1

The trail had to be right here. If I could find that creek I remembered leaping across — but all I could see was more brush and house-size boulders. Overhead, hidden somewhere in the huge fir branches, a bird called. High, panicky squawks that drove right through me.

Help! Help me, someone! Come back and find me!

I looked back down the valley of blazing white granite and evergreen trees. On both sides were giant, snowcapped mountains and behind them a row of even higher, snowy ridges. Mountains everywhere. An awesomely blue sky; white, heapy clouds. And me. All alone.

Lost. Temporarily. The sweat dripped down into my eyes, cold sweat. I could feel my heart kicking like a hoof under my padded backpack strap. Temporarily, it had to be temporarily! Just keep your head, Bennet girl, you'll find the trail, you probably aren't really even lost. My boot slipped on a loose rock about the size of a football and I sat down with a thud on icy granite, my big pack banging against my aching neck, my throat shut tight. Just keep your head, I told myself. You'll find the trail. You've got to find the trail!

This so-called trail over the glary granite was marked only with little piles of stones every twenty feet or so. Our teacher told us they were called "ducks." They were awfully hard to see against all the other white rock.

The others couldn't be that far ahead! I only sat down to rest by that last marker for a second!

And that's when it happened — my heart almost ground to a full stop again when I thought of it — I saw something brown in the brush on the other side of the trail, like a fur jacket, shining in the sun —

A bear was staring at me from the bushes. A huge bear. My mother's face swam in front of me. How sad she was going to be when she heard I was dead! The bear parted the bushes and stepped out on the trail. He was enormous.

She was enormous. Beside the bear was

a cub that, seen safely through cage bars, I would have called cute. *The most dangerous bears are mothers with cubs.* Mr. Quillan had said that. He had also said that the California black bears wouldn't attack humans. They would steal your food if they could, but they didn't want confrontations any more than we did.

But these bears weren't black. They were cinnamon brown and so close I could see their glittery eyes. The big trees, the clouds, the sky, everything was sucked up and overturned in front of me.

Play dead, a voice shouted in my mind. Protect your face! I curled up in as much of a ball as I could with that big pack on, pulled up my knees, hid my head in my chest between my hands, and prayed it would be over soon. Everything inside my head seemed to come loose, like lumps of ice joggling in a black sea.

It was a while before I realized I was still alive. I waited another hour, it seemed, before cautiously raising my head enough so I could open one eye.

The bears were gone; I didn't stick around to see more. I scrambled to my feet and whammed off up the mountain as fast as I could, going around big boulders, running over granite faster and faster, crossing that little stream, alive, alive! —

wait till I told the others — until I realized I wasn't on the trail.

I rushed back down the slope of granite, calling as loudly as I could, but no one was in sight. I ran back and forth, praying I would see that little pile of stones, the duck I had rested by.

Or any duck marking the trail.

Lost. Lost! What had made Mr. Quillan appoint me as a rear leader? Did he think getting B's in math qualified me as a mountaineer? And what dumb vanity had made me accept? Idiot, idiot, idiot! Showing off for my friends, that's what it was.

And where were those friends who promised they would take care of me in these horrible mountains? The friends who had talked me into this monster trip?

The whistle! On a string around my neck — I yanked it out and blew three times, remembering how we'd joked when Mr. Quillan had passed out whistles on the bus. Three blasts, that's the SOS signal in the mountains, he had told us back in San Francisco, reminded us at the trailhead, and told us again last night at dinner.

"People get lost in the Sierra every summer." The ominous words came back to me. "Some of them are never seen again." Only last year a girl had wandered out of one of the high camps in Yosemite to take some pictures after supper and had disappeared. They never even found her body. "If you have an accurate compass, bring it," he urged. Naturally I didn't have a compass. Who needs a compass in the city? I assumed I would be with the others, and they would know the way.

Never drop behind the rear leader, he'd ordered us. But I *was* the rear leader!

If I'd had any idea I'd be left alone out here with wild bears, I would have chained myself to a wheel of the bus! I would have flung myself down and locked my arms around Quack Quillan's knees and begged him to let me go home. And I wouldn't have cared a rap if Phillip Hargrove was watching, which he certainly wouldn't be.

They had to come for me! Soon! Before the bears came back!

A person could die from getting as scared as this. I got shakily to my feet and blew my whistle again, a shrill *threep! threep! threep!*

There's no more terrifying sound than the silence in the wilderness after you call and no one answers.

The big patches of snow under the trees and the mats of white flowers in the sun were beginning to be striped with very dark shadows. Night comes quickly in the mountains, Mr. Quillan had told us. My hands were cold, I realized, getting numb with cold, and I had no matches. Back in San Francisco, Mr. Quillan had stressed the fact that we must all carry matches. I didn't see why twenty-five kids needed matches for one fire, so I hadn't bothered. I wouldn't know how to make a fire, anyway.

It can get below freezing at night, he had said.

Somebody has to come back and find me!

The most lonesome wind in the world stirred the big branches of the trees. Up ahead the granite side of the mountain glittered back, as if mocking me.

I got my whistle to my mouth again, but I was crying too hard to blow it.

Chapter 2

We had been walking home from school, a safe, normal May afternoon, when it all started.

"Craziest idea you've had yet, Darcie," I had said. "I hate camping. You hate camping. Off in the Sierra with Mr. Quillan, Quack Quillan, of all the teachers! What sort of bozos will sign up to go camping with him?"

"Not camping, girl. Backpacking! And let me tell you what kind of bozos." Darcie actually licked her lips. "Phillip Hargrove, that's who."

"Darcie, Darcie." It was really pathetic, this crush she had on a boy who didn't know she was alive.

"Do it for me, Bennet. We'll have a blast. Why shouldn't we try something new for a change? A challenge. Ken says he'll arrange to get the packs and sleeping bags and stuff we'll need."

That made me like the idea even less. Darcie's brother, Ken, who's going to be a junior at Lowell — he's one year ahead of us — is a private problem of mine. One day he looked up from his computer and got imprinted with me, the way those gray goslings did in the experiment? The first thing they saw that moved they figured was Mother. I was the first girl Ken really focused on — he's heavily into his computer — and that was it. He's far too shy to ever say anything and that's good, because I'd die before I'd hurt his feelings. But I don't like to let him do things for me. Slavish devotion makes you feel so gross.

And I'm just your average, skinny, dishwater blonde. With funny teeth. My mother has spent a fortune on braces, but I still have windy little spaces between them. Darcie claims my rat teeth are sexy. "And you do have dynamite blue eyes," she says. That may be true, even though without my contacts I'm blind as a stone.

I was already fourteen and a half; it looked like I was going through life flat-chested. "Think of the money and washing I'll save on bras," I pointed out to Mom, who frowned. She didn't think it was nice to talk about things like that. Mom's big on *nice*.

"Your mom's so nice." Darcie must have been reading my thoughts. "Cleaning your room for you — and those sandwiches with the crusts trimmed off. Ironing your blouses. Knitting up any sweater you want practically overnight. She's the greatest." Darcie's mother works; she and Ken don't see too much of her.

"It's not so great the way she all but does my breathing for me. You know how I have to account for every minute of the day."

"She lets you go places; you only have to ask."

"And get the third degree of who, what, where, and why. If I'm not home on the stroke — you know how early *that* always is — she'd probably call the police. And the FBI. And the President."

I'd given up arguing with Mom. I thought next year, when I would be a sophomore, I could get through to her.

My dad died years ago and Mom dedicated herself to me. He was the one who named me Bennet, after one of Jane Austen's heroines. Personally, I think it's a very classy name. He was an English professor, my father.

"Bennet, can't you see it?" Darcie gurgled on. "Five days and five nights on the same trip with *him*?"

"Some trip. The country. I hate it out there! Nothing but lots of boring old trees and boring old bushes. And bugs, Darcie. Poison oak. Mud." Of course I knew Mom would never let me go backpacking in the wilderness, even with a teacher in charge of the trip. I wasn't worried.

I'm a city person myself; I love San Francisco as much as any tourist from Wisconsin. The shiny swoops of our bridges across the bay, Fisherman's Wharf, the cable cars, those gray walls of fog rolling in from the Pacific, and the kind of sad honking of the foghorns.

I especially adore Golden Gate Park, where Darcie and I were walking that day. We were cutting behind the Japanese Tea Garden to get to our bus stop. The cherry blossoms were out of bloom, but a million other things were filling the air with color and dreamy smells. It was warm and sunny, with cool, four o'clock shadows just starting across the shaved-looking grass. The fresh kind of day that puts you in an expectant mood. An on-the-brink-of-something day.

"I'm in no hurry to get home," I said, thinking of the stacks of math and history waiting to be done.

"I wonder what sort of snack she'll have today. Oh, I know it'll be good, even if it is nutritious," Darcie added loyally. Mom tended toward milk and carob brownies or stone-ground wheat crackers, laid out with ironed napkins. After one half hour exactly, she'd look at her watch and say, "It's time for Bennet to get to her homework." Darcie would leap right up — she really loves my mom and her rules. Her mother has to travel, and leaves Darcie and Ken on their own for days at a time. They don't have a father, either.

I would hit the books until Mom called me to a great dinner. She'd never let me help with the cleanup, either, but shooed me back upstairs to finish my homework, gab on the phone with my friends, or work on my drawings. I was doing an oil of our cat Gullie for Mom's birthday.

"Darcie, Mom will put the wipe on a backpacking trip in a hurry. And, aside from it being my idea of dull, is it really your thing? I mean, you're not exactly — well — athletic."

"Say it, Bennet. I'm a fat pig."

"Come on now. You've got everything going for you. What I wouldn't give for naturally wavy hair, like yours. And how many times do I have to tell you. Movie star eyes. That's what you've got!"

"But there's far too much of me, especially behind."

Some people wouldn't think so, but Darcie had made up her mind. Her brother is built the same way. And their mother? Ms. Stick Person. Wild.

"Baby fat," I told her instead, for the one million and forty-second time. "You'll be starting a great diet soon." She did that pretty often. "And when the boys see how gorgeous you really are — we should be working on what *I* could possibly do so they'll notice me. But I guess that's hopeless." To tell the truth I wasn't worried about boys yet; I was just trying to cheer up Darcie.

"Your mom might have fig cookies for us, like she did last week?" Obviously Darcie wasn't ready to diet again.

I went back to the trip idea. "Seriously, can you imagine my mom letting me go to the wilderness? I mean, come on."

"Well." She realized she hadn't thought this through. "But it *is* our official freshman class trip. It would be good for both of you, if you ask me."

"It would be good for Mom to loosen the old grip, I can see that, all right." I sighed. "But what about me? What good could it possibly do me, mucking around in the high Sierra? I bet the snow is still twenty feet deep up there."

"You're not listening. Mollie got it from Dee, who saw the sign-up sheet. Phillip Hargrove is definitely going."

"Libby Lou, too, then." Phillip and Libby Lou gave a new dimension to the words "going steady." You never, never saw Libby Lou without Phillip except in the girls' john. The King and Queen of Cool. They both lived in Sea Cliff, the ultra part of town, each house a big deal set in a rolling lawn, and we're talking here homes in a crowded city. If you wanted to know what Mrs. Hargrove wore to the opera opening, all you had to do was look in the newspaper the next morning.

There are a lot of rich kids at our school but just as many not rich ones like Darcie and me, whose families save on something else so we can go to a good, solid school where college prep, meaning tons of homework and strict discipline, is what it's all about. Parties and fun time are really played down. The freshman class gets one function per year, and you see the kind of thing they come up with. A five-day backpacking trip.

We had to wear school uniforms, too. Green-plaid pleated skirts, tailored white blouses, green blazers with baby blue piping on the collar and pockets. The boys wear dark green cords and white shirts, and get this, *ties*. They're really rigid at Bonwell Academy.

Darcie waved away the thought of Libby Lou as if Libby Lou didn't have silky blonde hair and the best figure in the freshman class. "Admit it, Bennet. Phillip Hargrove is the classiest boy in our entire school. Maybe any school in northern California," Darcie breathed.

He is tall, with a build, and kind of tumbling brown curly hair that makes his jaw look even more clean-cut and macho. "It's true he has a really awesome profile," I admitted. "But he's never even spoken to you. Saying 'hi there' in the hall doesn't count and you know it." There are only about 150 kids in Bonwell so we all know each other by sight.

"Let's ask Mom if you can stay and do math with me," I said, as we passed the museum where I used to take art lessons on Saturday. I've always wanted to be a textile designer. Of course, the very best place to study would be Cooper Union in New York City, but I knew I'd never have the nerve to go off alone to school like that, even if Mom would let me, which she never would.

Instead of nodding, Darcie stopped dead in her tracks and made a queer little sound in her throat.

Phillip Hargrove was running full blast out of the museum. I almost didn't recognize him because Libby Lou was nowhere in sight.

"Speak to him," Darcie hissed desperately. It was obvious she was in no shape to speak herself.

"Oh, honestly." What the heck, if it would make her happy. "Hi there," I called out, but in a high-pitched squeak, like a tiny child. Darcie's fault, making me self-conscious about a guy I couldn't care less about!

He shot right on by us, down the street, as if we were invisible.

We looked at each other. "Did you see that?" I asked. "Your beloved has just cut us dead in the water! Darcie! How can you go for anyone so gross?"

She moaned and giggled at the same time, which was just as pathetic as it sounds. "Maybe he didn't hear you," she offered unconvincingly at last. She giggled again. "I've never heard your voice so high. Hey, at least he was alone. I don't see Libby Lou anywhere."

"*She* would have spoken to us." In unison we did our Libby Lou imitation. "Dar-

CEE! Ben-NET! How AH you chaps?"
Libby Lou spent last year at a boarding
school in England and she's not about to let
anyone forget that. She has no time for us,
which is not a problem.

"Sea Cliff snobs," I said.

"Sea Cliff stuck-ups," Darcie echoed, but
her round cheeks kind of trembled, and I
felt a twinge. She did have a thing for that
boy. I had to at least try to help; she would
have done the same for me.

"Oh, all right," I said. "I will ask my
mother if I can go on this freaky trip with
you and your extremely gross fixation. She
won't let me go, but for you I'll ask her."

"Bless you," Darcie breathed. "Oh Bennet, can't you see it? Us up there in the
wilderness with Phillip Hargrove!"

"And Libby Lou. And Quack Quillan;
don't forget him. And everyone else
whacked out enough to sign on. Darcie, if
this went through we would suffer, suffer,
suffer."

"School trips can be a lot of fun," Darcie
said firmly. "Wholesome, clean, teacher-
supervised fun. Educational. Enriching.
Let's go try it on your mother."

"*Why* am I so nice?" I whimpered melo-
dramatically as the bus came and we
boarded. I wasn't worried. I would have bet

my newest tapes that I wasn't going anywhere near any wilderness. Knowing a
stuck-up like Phillip Hargrove was in the
group made it even less appealing.

If possible.

Chapter 3

But you just can't tell about life. Darcie had no more than started her pitch that day when I heard my uptight mother say thoughtfully, "Bennet has never been to the Sierra, really. Once we went to Camp Handy years ago, when her father was alive. You probably don't remember that, honey."

"Oh, yes, I do. I remember how the pool was over-chlorinated, and my eyes stung for weeks. And we had to go do dumb crafts every baking-hot afternoon. I'll never forget how glad I was to come home."

"This is backpacking, Mrs. Kinnell," Darcie explained. "We'll carry everything we need with us. Sleeping bags, food, extra clothes. My brother says he'll loan me all his stuff and he'll borrow from his friend for Bennet. We'll have a blast."

"It's a five-day trip, Mom. Five days and five nights." I said, spelling it out. She wouldn't be able to survive that long, worrying about me. Who would tell me to brush my teeth? Who would make my bed for me? Not that there would be any beds, I realized. The group would be lying out there in the woods, exposed to the freezing cold. Wild animals would step over everyone in the night. Bears! I shuddered. "Actually, I don't really want to go all that much."

Darcie gave me a heartbroken look.

"But it's up to you, Mom," I said loyally. "Maybe it would be good for you."

"Mother!"

"Let's think about it a little, honey."

Darcie broke out in a big smile. I could almost see her fantasy of Phillip Hargrove revolving in her head, looping around like a string of flashy Christmas lights. What I couldn't figure out was what was going on in my mother's overprotective mind.

Later, as she was wiping the kitchen counters after dinner, it began to fall into place. "Gran called this afternoon."

"Oh, I wish I'd been here!" My grandmother is a neat, neat lady. She's traveled everywhere, and keeps on traveling. She's kind of famous, in fact — a photographer in the Vietnam war. We have the picture she took of President Johnson with Thieu. She's just a fabulous person.

Outspoken, too. She's always after my mother to stop babying me so much.

"She's invited you to go to Europe with her this summer."

I gave a great yell, but Mom's look stopped me.

"Honey," she said uncomfortably, "I just can't let you go for a whole summer. When you're eighteen, maybe you could have a long trip like that. But instead, let's think about this school outing. I must untie the apron strings, she says. That I do too much for you. But I want you to have a happy, carefree time while you're young."

Frankly, I think that's because my mother didn't have a happy, carefree time when she was young. When she was my age, Gran was taking foreign assignments and Mom was left to keep house for her father and older brother.

"I'm not hanging on to you, am I? Bennet, if you want to go on this trip, you just go." Gullie rubbed against her ankle and she picked up the cat. Gullie's old and fat and drives Mom mad by shedding everywhere, but Mom spoils her rotten.

"Mom, it's all right. Darcie's the one who wants to backpack."

She wasn't listening. "Gran could be right. You should have a trip, on your own. But not the whole summer!"

"It's okay, Mom. If I can't go to Europe, I don't want to go anywhere, really." But I could see her conscience was bothering her. She was determined to let me go somewhere. I began to feel just the tiniest bit alarmed.

Before I could begin to convince her how much I didn't want to go backpacking, the phone rang. Dee was calling about the trip. She and Mollie were definitely going and I just had to come with them! We would have such a good time, the four of us together! Dee's a hyper little redhead with yellow eyelashes and lots of freckles.

"But you have to lug heavy packs," I pointed out. "That's fun, making like a burro?"

"We'll carry part of your stuff. Bennet, we'll baby and pamper you just like your own mother."

"Creepy things will crawl over me in the night." I shuddered at the thought.

"No, no. You'll be sleeping inside Ken's tent. Darcie says she's borrowing it." She hadn't wasted any time getting Dee to work on me.

"We'll freeze to death. There's twenty feet of snow on the ground."

"Not where we're going. It's all melted at Thunder Lake," Dee said. "You're such a baby, honestly."

And so, like a real dum-dum, I agreed to sign on with my crazy, fearless friends.

"That's lovely, dear. You'll have a wonderful time," Mom said. But when I kissed her good-night that evening we clung to each other for a second. She was wishing the trip was over as much as I was.

What had I done?

At least I had made Darcie happy. Looking back, even now, I'm glad about that. Her face positively shone when we filed into room 101 after school the next week to be oriented for the trip by Mr. Quillan, our math and science teacher.

Quack Quillan, as he's known behind his back. He does toe out when he walks, just like Donald, and his teeth (I always notice people's teeth) kind of stick out in a shelf. I guess they didn't have orthodontics when he was young. It's not that he isn't a good guy; he practically cries when he has to give someone a low grade. I know. I had to spend fifteen minutes comforting him when he broke the news to me that I was messing up in math. He kept looking down at his shoes, quacking under his breath in real misery. In fact, he urged me to come in after school for private tutoring, which I did.

"You just turned the old baby blues on him," Dee accused.

Of course I wouldn't try anything on a teacher! But he was very helpful; I passed his course with a solid B. It's just that the poor guy is disorganized. He walks around, toeing out, in a dream half the time.

It was the high Sierra he was probably dreaming about, I realized at the meeting. His face cleared, he rapped out information like a drill sergeant, he had the answer to every question. A backpacking maniac.

"Bennet." Darcie gave me a poke. "Look who isn't here."

Phillip Hargrove had come in and sat down. Alone. I looked back twice to make sure. It was perfectly true. Libby Lou was not at the meeting.

Did I say Darcie's face shone before? Now it practically blinded everyone in our row.

"Libby Lou could still be coming on the trip."

Darcie kept right on smiling.

"He is a stuck-up, a snob," I reminded her. "Have you forgotten how he snubbed us?"

Darcie kept right on smiling.

While Mr. Quillan quacked eagerly on about breakfast and dinner being commissary meals, bring your own lunches, the bears aren't a problem if you hang your food right, the news went around the room. Libby Lou Driscoll was not, repeat, *not* going on the class trip.

"I'll never figure out why," Darcie said between smiles, poking her pencil in her dark hair.

"No mystery to me," I snarled. "She's got more sense than we gave her credit for."

"Bennet! You're going to love it. You'll see!" Darcie, Dee, and Mollie kept it up. "Listen, let's go together tomorrow to get our boots. We'll all go practice hiking this weekend on Mount Tam!" That's a humongous mountain across the Golden Gate in Marin County.

Sunday Darcie, Dee, Molly, and I caught the bus to Mount Tam. We went everywhere together. Of course Darcie was my *best* best friend, ever since second grade. She and I used to pretend that we were sisters.

I began to think the trip might not be too bad, especially with Darcie and the others right there with me. The meadows and everywhere were covered with golden poppies as big as tulips and all kinds of blue and red and yellow flowers. We saw five deer, every one like Bambi. The trails were deep dirt paths with signposts all over the place. Naturally I assumed all trails were like that. *And* I didn't get a single blister from my new hiking boots. All day we had a ball, giving Darcie really tough advice on how to get Phillip Hargrove to notice her on the trip. She just smiled on. But Mollie, who's tall and loose-jointed with a great mane of black hair, really tried to get through to her.

"Remember Stretch, Darcie?" Mollie asked, and we all sighed.

Darcie looked at her, honestly puzzled. She had forgotten all about Stretch, even though last year she had made herself sick yearning over him. Stretch Dickinson, our basketball star. Six six, chinless — the Big Bird profile? It was after Stretch transferred out of Bonwell that Darcie turned on to Phillip Hargrove, a huge leap up aesthetically, but even more hopeless.

"At least Stretch would talk to you in the lunchroom sometimes," Mollie pointed out. Phillip never had eyes for anyone but Libby Lou.

But there was no getting to Darcie.

"It's possible we might survive this mad adventure," I admitted grudgingly to them after the hike, as we sat wedged in a booth devouring pizza. The open air gives one a roaring appetite, an important fact I wish I had remembered.

Poor Darcie. She didn't get the chance to find out.

The very morning we were to leave — we had to be in front of school at noon sharp — her brother called.

"Bad news, Bennet." Ken's voice is so shy you have to listen carefully. "Darcie's got some kind of bug; she's running a fever." She had seemed a little off the day before, refusing for once to come home with me for a snack after school, saying she had to check her packing again. I had put it down to the excitement of the trip.

"We've decided she can't come." "We" meant he and Darcie; their mother was in Los Angeles all that week on some deal. "The doctor's coming out."

"A housecall?" I knew then it was serious. "Ken! How's she taking it?"

"Badly. Very badly. She says her last chance in life is passing her by. I keep telling her the mountains will be there for another zillion years. Hold on, I'll take the phone to her bed."

She could barely croak. "My last chance in life — "

"Darcie, it's not that big a deal. But I'm not going to go without you."

"Bennet," I could hardly hear her, "you've got to go! Please, for me, go and keep tabs on *him* —"

"No! It'll be horrible without you. Even with Dee and Mollie, I'd be so scared."

There was a heartbroken little sniffle at the other end. "Please."

I broke down. "Okay, okay. Just for you, I'll carry on." I realized I had to now, anyway; it was too late to drop out. Those expensive boots and everything. "I'll get out there and experience it all in-depth for both of us. I'll take notes on your beloved. Oh, I know how much you want to go! I'd give anything if we could just trade places for the next week."

That statement really came back to haunt me.

Chapter 4

All the way up to the mountains Mollie and Dee and I mourned Darcie's rotten luck.

"She might even have gotten to know him." Dee dropped her voice to a whisper. "After all, Libby Lou isn't here to fence him off."

"He doesn't look exactly lonely," I pointed out. "Do you really need to whisper?" Phillip Hargrove was sitting ten rows ahead on the bus and seemed to be having a great time, laughing loudly with some of the other Sea Cliff crowd. Mostly boys. As a matter of fact, the ratio of girls to boys on that bus was beautiful. And worrying. What did the other girls know about backpacking that we didn't know and were going to find out?

Five whole days. Five whole nights. What was I doing on that bus?

But so far it was nonthreatening. The closer we got to the mountains the bluer the sky got. Finally we stopped at a fast-food place for dinner.

Phillip Hargrove and his friends were in line right behind us. I was getting tired of being so aware all the time of Darcie's old beloved.

Especially when Mollie and Dee got cute.

"We'll make a report on its physical activities." Mollie rolled her big brown eyes archly toward Phillip.

"Total tonnage? Input and output?" Dee asked her, and they exploded into giggles.

It wasn't that hilarious. I was glad Phillip was so busy with his friends that he hadn't heard them.

"Are we talking twenty-four-hour coverage here?" Mollie went on, between snickers. "It's the least we can do for poor Darcie."

Luckily we were at the counter by then and had to give our orders. We took our trays of burgers and shakes to an empty booth.

"I say Bennet for the first shift." One thing about Mollie, she's persistent. Unfunny, but persistent. "Then I'll take over at midnight, and Dee — " She stopped and choked on a mouthful of hamburger.

"Is this place taken?" Phillip was standing over us, even favoring us with a slight, maybe his second-best, smile. "There's no room for me in there." His friends were sprawled all over the booth ahead.

"No! Sure! Sit!" Mollie gasped, crumbs spraying.

He gave her a curious look before turning his back on all of us, leaning over the booth to continue his conversation with his buddies.

We sat studying the back of his head. Very wavy, shiny brown hair.

"Remember this for Darcie," Mollie ordered us in a whisper. "If only she were here!"

"We wouldn't have had an empty place if she'd been here," I whispered back sourly.

The girls kept looking reverently at Phillip's back.

Mr. Quillan began to shout for everyone to be on the bus in five minutes. To my surprise Phillip swung back around. He smiled, being gracious to the lower orders. Up close he really wasn't all that handsome, I decided. His eyes were a sharp hazel green; I hadn't noticed that before. But then it had been hard to get a good look, with Libby Lou always flashing around him like a strobe light. "Nice sharing a booth with you girls."

"If that's what you call it," I murmured and headed for the rest room.

Back on the bus, Mr. Quillan stood up and blew his whistle. When everyone quieted down, he gave us another lecture on how to conduct ourselves in the wilderness. He passed out whistles and warned us not to take a step on the trail without them around our necks. There was a lot of wise-mouthing.

"You don't have to worry, Bennet," Dee said. "I've promised, cross my heart, to look out for you."

"Me, too," Mollie said. "I took the solemn pledge from — "

"When did she get to you?" I could just hear Mom: " — feel so much better if you'd keep an eye on Bennet. She doesn't realize — " Mom meant, my daughter doesn't have the sense to come in out of the rain. She's two years old and backward. . . . I don't think my mother even *knew* what she did to me. I groaned.

We were definitely getting into the Sierra now. The road twisted around higher and the mountains began to get very woodsy and rocky. And cold. We all got out our down jackets and wool caps. I didn't care for the look of those peaks, all snow and blue shadows, very Himalaya-ish and sinister. The others snapped pictures.

The sunset was a total experience. We had to turn around in the bus to take it all in — the whole west splashed over with bloody reds and every cloud we could see dyed pink. More pictures were taken.

We made a last rest stop in the tiny town of Three Streams, and then there was nothing but trees and rocks and us. Just about dark we rolled into our campground at the head of the trail we were to take the next day.

Mr. Quillan blew his whistle. The girls, all nine of us, were to spread out our sleeping bags on one side of the bus and the sixteen boys on the other. "No tents necessary tonight, class," he said blissfully. "Tonight we sleep under the stars!"

There were two terrible pit toilets back in the woods. No water. Not a drop. "I reminded everyone to fill canteens at Three Streams," Mr. Quillan told me reproachfully. "You'll have to get water from the creek over there." He pointed to a dark, evil-looking clump of trees. "And purify it, Bennet. You do have your tablets?"

Good old Dee brought her flashlight and came to the stream with me.

"What a dumb camp," I sputtered as we knelt down by the water. "Don't you think they'd have at least one little faucet?"

A huge shape detached itself from the

mass of shadows and clumped toward us.

Dee squealed and I dropped my canteen with a clatter.

"Faucets. Why not hot showers and microwave ovens?" The shape laughed scornfully and became Phillip Hargrove. "Hey, did I scare you girls?"

"No, no," I said frostily. "We always jump and scream a little when we're thirsty."

"If you're thirsty you better fill your canteen. Here, let me." He found my canteen and filled it along with his. "Do you know how to purify?"

"Of course I know." I snatched my canteen from him, and we started back.

"Don't forget to wait twenty minutes after you put the tablets in," he called after us.

"Make a note for Darcie," I said grimly to Dee. "Her beloved is very bossy."

Mollie had spread out a big tarp for us to put our pads and sleeping bags on. "You go in the middle, Bennet."

"So you two can keep your motherly eyes on me." But I was glad to scoot down between them.

We stared up at the stars. I had never seen stars like that before, so big and flashy, and there were jillions of them. Then the boys on the other side of the bus began to sing and we joined in. It didn't seem so lonely with all those voices going. We sang up a storm, but after a while Mr. Quillan cut us off. "There are other people camping here, class," he boomed from his sleeping bag over with the boys. "The rule is no noise after ten o'clock."

"I had no idea there were so many rules and regulations in the wilderness," I said to Dee, who yawned and grunted. The girl was actually falling asleep in her sleeping bag.

So was Mollie. I felt very much alone. There was something hard and lumpy under my back. I tried moving over to the left, but I discovered that I could only move by hitching the bag along with me. It took a monster effort.

I tried counting sheep, but the sheep were wearing backpacks and jumping one by one off a horrible cliff. I was sure something was crawling on my leg and sat up whimpering, checking through the sleeping bag inch by inch. I didn't find it. Melancholy thoughts about all the gross things that could slither right into my sleeping bag swept over me. Snakes. Rats. Bats. Tarantulas. I pulled the strings of the bag so tightly around my face that my head began to ache.

A wind started up, and I could see the tops of the giant pines waving against the stars. I tried again to find the Big Dipper. Mollie began to snore, little, soft, kitten snores that made me think of our cat Gullie at home and my mother. I hoped Mom had been able to go to sleep.

Crash! It came from the woods and I sat up, my heart thumping. Bears. Bears were coming to attack us! I waited for Mr. Quillan to wake up and save us! No one stirred. There was no more crashing, and after a while I was able to weakly lie down again.

The moon came up from behind the trees, big and bald as a balloon, making me feel more exposed than ever. Everyone else in the world was fast asleep. I tried counting sheep again. How was I going to hike all those miles tomorrow, lugging a heavy pack, if I didn't get some sleep?

A motorcycle roared down at the other end of the campground, and I heard some loud laughing. Not everyone obeyed the no-noise rule, obviously. Then I felt a cold clutch in my stomach.

Motorcycles. A gang! They would attack us as we slept. It was a good thing I, at least, was awake, but what should I do? I lay there listening to the talk and laughter, debating about yelling out to wake up Mr.

Quillan. As long as they were partying down there we were all right here, I decided, but I must stay awake....

I awoke with a start, and realized I had dozed off. A light sound had awakened me. I heard it again.

Footsteps. Coming this way. I moved cautiously around, until I was sitting up in my bag among the sleeping girls.

A figure was coming toward us.

The motorcycle gang. Attacking. I reached over and poked Mollie sharply.

"Ohh," she groaned sleepily. "What's going on?"

"Don't make a sound," I hissed. "There's someone coming this way!"

"Bennet, honestly," she began, but I clapped my hand over her mouth.

"Shh, he'll hear you! Sit up and see for yourself."

Mollie propped herself up on an elbow.

"Out there!" I whispered. "By that tree. Where is Mr. Quillan?"

"Out there. That *is* Mr. Quillan, you dork."

I peered again through the darkness and recognized the outward waddling feet.

"Probably had to go to the john. Bennet, honestly. You'll be a total wreck by morning if you keep this up." Mollie was practically asleep before she finished talking.

I must have lost consciousness for a few minutes at least, because I woke up, and it was light. There was dew on our sleeping bags and it was very cold. We made short work of getting our jeans and boots back on.

"If only Darcie were here," we sighed to each other at breakfast. She would have loved crowding around the picnic table, rubbing elbows with her beloved. The boys got a roaring fire going, and Mr. Quillan scrambled up a huge mess of eggs for our breakfast. He had told us to bring our own lunches, but the other two meals were group affairs. Everyone who wanted to (which didn't include me) had pitched in to cook this morning, but from now on meal chores would be assigned.

We all sat around eating in the sunshine, some of us sitting at empty picnic tables, others on stumps or big rocks. I found myself tracking Phillip's movements, which was very annoying. Even though I was doing it for Darcie, I felt like I was turning into some kind of groupie.

Loathsome mosquitoes began to dive bomb us, and we slathered on mosquito repellent. The clever mosquitoes then went for our plates of scrambled eggs, like living pepper fluttering on the yellow chunks.

I dumped my plate in the tall grass. "If

only Darcie were here. She'd lose at least five pounds a day. We're going to be living skeletons when we get back. If we get back."

"Oh, Bennet, honestly. You're such a baby," the girls said, almost automatically. "Forget the mosquitoes. Look at the fabulous view." Their eyes were trained on Phillip and his buddies scrubbing down the table. He was wearing a red bandanna around his wavy brown hair, an Indian warrior touch that would have broken Darcie in two.

The girls helped me get my sleeping bag stuffed, pad rolled up, and both of them hitched to my pack, before we went to get our share of the food to carry. Mr. Quillan had arranged it all on the picnic table. Some of the boys showed off by grabbing the biggest, heaviest things. I tested out the various bags and came away with the lightest.

"Wait, Bennet," Mr. Quillan called from the bus, which he was locking. "That big pot goes with the oatmeal, since it weighs so little."

The girls giggled, but they helped me cram it all in my pack.

Finally everyone was ready. There was no getting out of it now. Mr. Quillan, after commenting happily on the perfect weather, gave yet another little talk. It was six easy miles to Hunters' Lake for the first night — we should get there by mid-afternoon. Then we could set up our tents, look at the birds and flowers, fish, and so on.

Mr. Quillan swung into an update on Safety in the Woods. He was really hung up on the subject. "And now," he cleared his throat, "I have appointed an assistant leader." No one was surprised when he announced his name: Phillip Hargrove. "We'll need a rear leader, too." Mr. Quillan looked around us, his glasses flashing blissfully. "Remember, no one falls behind the rear leader. It's his responsibility to see there are no stragglers." Then his face changed, and I could see a thought forming: not he, *she*. Equality here in the woods. He caught my eye. "Bennet, would you serve as our rear leader?"

Mollie and Dee hoo-hooed right out loud, and so did a few of the others. There was a kind of amused sneer, I thought, on Phillip Hargrove's face.

"I'd love to, Mr. Quillan." What else could I have said? Anyway, everyone knew there was nothing to rear leading, which was probably why he had given the job to a girl. What could be easier than being the last one? All I had to do was follow along behind the person in front.

But it wasn't that easy to keep up. My pack weighed a ton and rubbed my shoulders painfully. In the woods great clouds of mosquitoes attacked us, and Mr. Quillan had to call a halt so we could re-smear ourselves with repellent.

At first Mollie and Dee hiked loyally back with me and the Donavan twins, who were sauntering along at a snail's pace, *my* kind of pace, in front of us. But the girls decided it was their duty to hike ahead, within reporting distance of Phillip. "We'll see you when Quack calls a rest stop," they promised, and raced ahead.

Quack didn't call a rest stop. We plodded on through the woods, hour after hour. Trees, rocks, bushes, remnants of old snow. My legs, thighs, feet, and shoulders were burning. My neck felt like it was broken. I was grateful for the Donavan twins, who were going so slowly the ones ahead had to wait up periodically.

Luckily, someone spotted something in one of the patches of snow still under the trees, and Mr. Quillan halted the line so we could all gather around for a lecture on pinedrops. It's a saprophyte, he announced, which feeds only on decayed organic matter. A pathetic, kind of reddish stick flower that most people would hurry right on by. But I asked as many questions as I could think up to keep him stationary.

Mr. Quillan was thrilled. "I'm glad Bennet is taking advantage of this trip to learn all she can about the wilderness. The Sierra is a fragile environment, class, and the more we know, the better able we'll be to protect it, preserve it for our children and their children to enjoy." He was off on ecosystems. We got another five minutes' rest.

For hours we mushed on. Just when I was positive my knees were going to buckle under me and I would fall in the path, never to get up again, salvation! Mr. Quillan called for a lunch stop.

I barely took the time to find Mollie and Dee before I wiped the sweat out of my eyes and attacked my lunch, eating almost half of it before I saw what I was doing. It was now clear that I hadn't packed enough food for this trip. I hadn't realized working like a mule would do gross things to my appetite.

"Don't worry," Dee said, cramming in more cheese and crackers. "I've brought tons and that's just what it feels like. Tomorrow you can take some of mine, and lighten my load."

"We're behind schedule, class," Mr. Quillan told us. "We've got to get to camp in case those clouds develop into something." He gave a worried look at the sky, which now featured fluffy little clouds.

I know no more than fifteen minutes passed before he was blowing his whistle to get us back on the trail. That afternoon was a blur of aching muscles as we moved upward, the only direction there seemed to be in the mountains. About every twenty minutes the group had to stop for the Donavan twins and me; I had the impression that Phillip Hargrove was glaring at me each time. I didn't care. It was all I could do to keep going. Up the line I heard some of the kids laughing and joking. Evidently they actually enjoyed this torture. Or pretended to.

My head was aching now, too, but I knew that was from the altitude combined with lack of sleep. Mr. Quillan had told us we might feel some slight effect from the altitude, but our bodies would soon adjust. "We're not going to be high enough for altitude sickness to be a problem. The really high country, eleven and twelve thousand feet, is still buried under snow. We can't get in there this early." He had actually sounded sorry about it.

Hunters' Lake turned out to be a lovely, emerald green, set dramatically into the granite. I tottered over and sank down next to Mollie and Dee. I was beyond appreciating the scenery.

Before we could really get into resting Mr. Quillan came along. "Get your tents up, girls! We've gotten in so late we must set up camp right away." The sun was getting low.

I dug Ken's tent out of my pack. "How am I going to get this up?" I wailed. "Darcie was the one who knew how!" Not only did I long for Darcie, but I had a sneaking wish my mother were also there to help me.

"Don't panic," Mollie said. "You can squeeze in with Dee and me. Safety in numbers."

"You dolls." I sank down on my pad to rest while they put their tent up.

"We've got to keep watch for Darcie," Mollie whispered, looking around for Phillip. I decided I didn't need to worry about what he thought of them tailing him. He was too blissed out to notice. There he was in the flashiest boots, carrying the most gigantic fishing pole I'd ever seen. Late as it was, he and his buddies were going to fish.

Mr. Quillan read off the chore roster for

evening. Mollie and Dee were on it, and had to get right to work, making the salad. They got up, groaning.

"Just be glad you didn't get some sleaze job, like KP," I consoled them. "But hurry it up. I can't remember ever being so hungry. Get cracking, you two."

Then I heard my name — "and Bennet Kinnell, cleanup after dinner."

It was their turn to laugh.

Chapter 5

The meal was delicious. Chili beans, coleslaw, brownies, and hot chocolate. I wasn't too tired to eat, and the girls weren't too tired to giggle about me having to do pots and pans.

"Probably the first time you've ever had to scrub a pot," Mollie kept saying. "Don't forget the rubber gloves."

I had just swallowed the last of my drink and was thinking seriously of asking for more, when I became aware of someone looming over me. Phillip Hargrove.

"We're on KP together." It sounded like an order the way he rapped it out.

Mollie and Dee gasped in unison.

I shrugged as if I'd known that all along. "I'll be there when I've finished my meal." He nodded and stomped away; Dee and Mollie stared at me openmouthed.

"Bennet, did you hear what you said?" "Talk about cool!" "Remember *everything* for Darcie!"

"He doesn't need to think he's going to boss me around," I said. I waited a good five minutes before I sauntered over to the cooking area, which was a giant hunk of granite. Phillip was heaving a great pot of water on the camp stove.

"Ooops!" I had raked a bunch of utensils off onto the ground.

We got down on our hands and knees to find them.

"Hey! You're dangerous!"

"Sorry! I didn't mean to!" He had backed right onto a big fork I'd just found.

"Relax. I don't feel any blood seeping out."

I was blushing all over. Spearing Darcie's beloved! I could just hear her. "Bennet! How could you be so *gross*!"

"I'm really sorry, Phillip."

He didn't answer as he got up. A Sea Cliff snob, I reminded myself.

"So where are the rubber gloves?" I intended to do my share. I hadn't done that many dishes, not with my mom in the kitchen, but I knew how.

"Rubber gloves!" Phillip gave me a really weird look. "You don't have any idea how to do this, do you?"

46

"But of course *you* do," I said sarcastically.

"Watch out while I pour this hot water. Use that scrubber thing there to wash," he ordered. He really had the idea he was in charge. "Quack shouldn't have chosen you for this job."

I stopped sloshing a stack of dishes into the sudsy water, amazed at his rudeness. "Too bad you didn't get to handpick your assistant!" I managed to gasp out. "If there's anyone here good enough!"

He looked at me seriously. "I just meant this is heavy work and you're kind of — well, frail-looking. I didn't mean you wouldn't do your best."

It was sort of an apology. I went to work with the dish mop. "Cheer up," Phillip said. "It's not a life sentence. We'll soon finish."

"Want to bet?" I would never admit it to a living soul, least of all Mollie and Dee, but he had a nice smile.

It did turn out to be hard work. After we got everything washed, we had to heat more water to scald them again. The other kids were singing around the camp fire. Phillip didn't say anything more. I wondered if he was thinking of Libby Lou — probably missing her.

It got dark before we finished. I had to

hold a flashlight while he fished in the rinse water for the last utensils.

"It's too bad we got in so late," I said. "If we'd eaten earlier, we would have been through with this in time for the singing."

Phillip stopped fishing. "It didn't occur to you we got here late because of you?"

"Me?" I guess my mouth dropped open.

"A good hour late, I'd say, because of you and the twins."

"That's not true!" I could hardly speak. Especially because I realized it *was* true. "How unfair of you to blame me!"

He shrugged. "People who aren't in shape for a hike should stay at home."

"People with big mouths should keep them shut!"

Phillip didn't answer. I wasn't about to say another word to him, ever. By this time Mr. Quillan had doused the camp fire and the kids were bedding down. How far away from home I was, and how much I wished this endless trip were over!

"Bennet, what's wrong?" Mollie asked anxiously as I stomped back to our tent and threw my boots viciously on the ground. "You better not leave your boots out there. What if it rains?"

"I'm thinking of the talk I've got to have with Darcie!" As we lay wedged in the tent I told the girls about Phillip. "He's

48

really *mean*. When she hears what he said to me, I'll bet she'll never speak to him again." I glossed over the fact that she never had actually spoken to him. They knew what I meant. "Bossy! He's really gross. And loathsome. If he weren't so stuck on himself, he'd see how ridiculous he is." I felt better saying all that, and hearing the girls agree.

I didn't have to do a chore for breakfast; we had pancakes and Tang. It was a gorgeous, clear day with only a few little clouds far away on the horizon. I felt stiff and sore as I loaded up. Every time I caught sight of Phillip I turned away. I didn't intend to speak to him again the whole trip. Mr. Quillan hadn't said anything to me about being too slow, so where did Phillip get off?

Dee and Mollie rushed to the head of the line again, still anxious to keep tabs on the beloved in spite of what I'd told them. I took up my place at the end. We walked through the woods, gradually going higher, and coming out of the trees onto a dazzling, white granite mountainside. As far as I could see it kept going up.

When we reached a tiny lake called Emerald Pool we stopped for lunch, and the true plan of the day was revealed, a twenty-minute lunch break for starters.

"We have five more miles to go to reach Thunder Lake today," Mr. Quillan announced, his glasses flashing in a worried way, "and there's climbing ahead this afternoon, class." If Quack Quillan didn't count what we did yesterday as climbing, what horrors lay ahead? Dee forgot to give me her extra lunch stuff and I didn't remind her. She was in better shape to carry it than I was.

And so, little guessing that the world as I knew it was shortly coming to an end, I tottered after the others.

I blame the Donavan twins. Whatever it was they had for lunch it should have been patented. They started up that mountain as if they were jet-propelled. I tried to speed up, too, but in a few minutes I was gasping, my chest felt like it was going to explode, and my eyes were blurred over with sweat.

"Hey, I've got to rest a minute," I shouted up to their climbing backs. "Tell Mr. Quillan I had to take a time-out, okay?"

They didn't turn around. Maybe they didn't hear me. I sank down by the trail marker to catch my breath for a second.

And then I saw the bears, stepping out on the trail. . . .

* * *

After my fit of crying, I felt a little better, even though nothing had changed. The wind still blew through the big fir branches above me, making a moaning sound, the boulders glittered in the sunlight, blue flowers waved underfoot, and I was still horribly, horribly alone.

Surely by now they had missed me and were coming back! Once more I put my whistle to my mouth and blew the signal, three short blasts, over and over. I didn't want to stop for fear I'd hear only that numbing silence again.

I heard the silence again. Panic climbed in my throat.

Action, okay, action! That's what I needed. It was getting too cold to sit on the stone any longer, anyway. I had to find that last marker! Once I found the trail I'd just wait there until they came. They might be there already.

Now clouds were covering the sun. It was definitely getting cold. I slipped out of my pack to get at my cap and mittens — and found I had forgotten to zip up the top compartment. My sun block, my extra sweater, my new red tights were gone! At least the cap and mittens were there. I put them on, hitched up my pack, and started back to find the stream I had rushed over.

How much longer would there be daylight? When I saw the sun again I would know where west was, I told myself. The sun goes down in the west, right? I can get my directions from that. And what good would that do? I answered myself back. I didn't know if the trail was west or east, or north or south. . . .

Don't think like that I said to myself sternly. The last marker was on the other side of that stream, right? So find the stream.

My mind tried to work. I couldn't have gotten more than a hundred yards from the trail, if that, before I realized I wasn't on it. They would find me. It might take a while — it might even get dark — my stomach lunged and I decided not to think about that. I couldn't handle the idea of being alone out here at night, even though I had my sleeping bag and Ken's tent. And no idea in the world how to put the tent up; I should have done it last night, instead of crawling in with the girls.

Then, about ten yards away, I saw a familiar-looking, enormous, gray boulder! On the other side of it, I should see that little stream, and then across from it —

No stream. More boulders, rocks, brush. And silence. My heavy breathing and the cold wind. I had less idea than ever where the trail was.

But surely they were looking for me!

By now the sky was covered with dark, angry-looking clouds. I stopped in a clearing and took off my pack again, too tired to cry anymore. I sat down on a log, unclipped my water bottle from my belt and had a good drink, before I remembered that until I found the stream that was all the water I had.

But it looked like soon I'd have more than enough water. It was going to rain. I took out some of the gorp Mom had made for me — a mixture of raisins, nuts, chocolate drops, and coconut — and made myself eat. I had to get my nerves under control.

Of course they were hunting for me now, looking and calling. Mr. Quillan must be going berserk. If the wind weren't making such a racket in the trees, I could probably hear them.

All I had to do was stay right here and they would find me. And the bears wouldn't? A few big, ploppy raindrops fell. I would have to have a go at putting up Ken's tent. If I could keep warm and dry, I had food and enough water to last until morning. But it was going to get very, very dark; I thought of all those creatures out there. Suppose I couldn't get the tent up, and the bears did find me. I couldn't swallow the gorp in my mouth.

How could this be happening to me? Me, Bennet, here alone in the wild mountains! Here on a rough, soggy log, lost, tired, and cold. Evening coming. Rain coming. And not a living thing around except wild bears. I made myself move those teeth, eat that gorp. I was going to need my strength.

I forced back tears, telling myself harshly that crying was a luxury I couldn't afford now. I had to stop sniveling and get to work on that tent. Serious raindrops were falling.

But I sat on, trying to reason it out and calm myself down. Mr. Quillan would hike straight to the trailhead and call the forest rangers, police, and everybody. But, a terrible little voice whispered, he won't be able to do that until morning, will he? Because it's already getting dark. And beginning to rain, hard.

Face it, I told myself. I'm going to be out here overnight. Tomorrow they'll start the search. Teams of people, dogs, helicopters. They'll find me. I would not think of that girl who wandered away from camp. She had fallen over a cliff or something, probably. *Me* they were going to find!

But they would have to tell my mother I was lost.

It was the thought of my mother's white, terrified face that undid me again. Tears slid down my cheeks, mixing with rain, and I just couldn't seem to get off that log. I jumped, though, at the first great rumble of thunder. And then I heard it.

On the ground, in the brush, something was coming.

I could heard the swish of branches being pushed aside, the heavy thuds — the bears!

It was one of those nightmares where you can't move; every effort is like pushing through dark, clutching molasses. It seemed to take hours, but in super-slow motion I got down behind the log, pulling my pack down on top of me, pressing my face in the damp earth. Please, I whispered out loud, oh, please, please!

The thuds came nearer. And then — the most beautiful, piercing sound I had ever heard, a whistle! And someone calling, "Bennet, Bennet!"

"Here! Over here, here I am!" The thunder crashed, lightning flashed — I knocked down my pack in my leap over the log, rushing straight toward that voice, finally reaching my rescuer. I crashed into his wonderful arms.

Phillip Hargrove had come back to find me.

Chapter 6

"Hey, it's okay! You're found!"

I was so happy! I didn't care that I was acting like an idiot, practically knocking Phillip over backward. He was the most beautiful sight in the world, like a big blue mountain in his poncho. I forgot totally that I had planned never to speak to him again.

"It seemed like I was lost for days. Weeks! Where are the others? I blew my whistle — no one came!" To my surprise more tears started down my face, even though I was safe now. I sat down on the log, shaking. "What luck you found me!"

"Not so hard, actually. You were just a little bit lost." He smiled down at me, pleased with himself. "You left a real trail." He handed me my sun block, sweater, red tights. "Litterbug."

"I didn't know my pack was unzipped — "

"I saw those red tights from the trail. When I reached them I saw the sweater — you really planted the clues."

I was too happy to be embarrassed. "You do know where the trail is?"

Lightning and thunder almost drowned out his words. "I'll lead you straight to it. But until this blows over we better take cover under that boulder over there."

He grabbed my pack and we crouched under the granite ledge. The rain began to pour down in sheets in front of us.

"Get your rain gear on," he commanded.

My fingers were so stiff it took me a while to undo the strings and haul out my rain jacket and pants. I pulled the jacket on, but I didn't have the strength or room to struggle into the pants. "Is Mr. Quillan mad?"

He hesitated. "I don't know. I came back to round you up on my own. I am the assistant leader, you know. I couldn't believe you'd leave the trail."

"I didn't go off the trail on purpose! Oh!" Lightning splintered right in front of us. "How long will it take us to get to the others?"

"They're not far ahead. But this won't let up for a while."

I didn't care. The most luscious warmth, like heated honey, seemed to be pouring through me, seeping into every cell of my body. I could have fallen asleep right there, crushed up against Phillip's slippery, cold poncho, too exhausted to even tell him about the bears. I'd been more tense and scared than I'd realized, even. But now I was safe, found and safe. What a story I was going to have for Mollie and Dee, to say nothing of Darcie!

There wasn't much room under that ledge. I could smell the chewing gum on his breath, a lovely, civilized, city smell.

"Phillip, how come you noticed I was missing?" I should have been ashamed of getting lost and causing all this trouble, but I was too happy to care. I didn't even care I would have to go on backpacking. After this killer of a day, the rest of it had to be a snap. I promised myself I would never get out of sight of another human being for the rest of the trip. Maybe for the rest of my life.

"It's my job to check, isn't it? I got the idea last night when we were on KP that you are — uh, reckless."

"Reckless? As well as slow?" He was starting on me again.

"Believe it. I've never been speared doing dishes before." He rubbed his back pocket and grinned. "Dangerous when armed. Quack Quillan will die when he finds out you left the trail. That's a stupid thing to do, Bennet."

"I didn't do it on purpose! I — " The lightning flashed again and I instinctively hid my head in my arms.

He laughed. Actually laughed at me. Which reminded me that he was a stuck-up snob I didn't care for.

"Don't worry, the lightning won't get you here."

"Well, I'm looking forward to leaving here. I want to be with the others." That sounded more gross than I'd planned, but I didn't say anything more, and neither did he. We watched the rain roaring down for a while. "But I thank you for coming back and finding me," I finally muttered.

"That's okay. I am the assistant leader."

"I'm really sorry I messed up your day," I said faintly, too tired suddenly to fight about it.

He looked at me with surprise. "Hey, don't take it personally."

"I do, though. I often take personally the way people act toward me." I remembered what he'd said to me the night before.

"I don't know what you're talking about. Listen, it looks to me like this rain is going to keep up for a while. And we're getting wet and cold, cramped in here. We've got to plan what to do."

"We're going back to the others! You said you know where the trail is!"

"I do. We are. But we can't go in a raging storm." Lightning cracked somewhere close by, and the trees lit up even through the thick rain. "We'd get fried! Don't you realize that? So, Bennet," he turned to me more formally, "do you have a tent?"

I stared at him. But I realized he was right. It was getting darker and colder. "Sure. Oh, you don't have your pack."

"Naturally I left it back up there on the trail, when I came to find you. I hope you've got plenty of food in yours."

"Gorp, my lunches. And a ton of oatmeal."

"Gorp will do it. But let's set up the tent first. It seems to have let up a little. How about that level place over by the tree?"

The thunder rumbled again. "We should put the tent up?" There's something terribly permanent about pitching a tent. I mean, it seemed to indicate we'd be spending the night in it. Phillip Hargrove and me. The girls and Darcie will simply die, I thought. I should take notes. "What happens when it gets really night?"

"When it gets really night we congratulate ourselves on having a warm, dry place to sleep. Especially me, without a sleeping bag."

"Oh! You can share mine — " I realized what I'd said and stared at him aghast. "Well, what I mean is. . . ." If I hadn't been so cold I guess I would have blushed.

He looked embarrassed, too. "I'll be fine in the tent; I've got my down jacket on under this poncho. Okay, so this is the tent?" He pulled a long brown bundle, a very heavy bundle, I might add, from my pack. "How do you put it up?"

"You don't know?" I thought pitching a tent was something all boys knew.

"*You* don't know? Hey, what's the point of bringing a tent you don't know how to set up?"

"My friend Darcie, who got sick and couldn't come, was going to handle the tent. You don't know who she is," I added pointedly.

He didn't get the point. "Of course I know Darcie. Real pretty girl. These must be the poles." There were two of them and lots of rope and peggy things. "For sure it doesn't work like mine." He studied the parts while I thought about how Darcie would pass out when I told her what the beloved thought about her.

"Okay. I think I know what the game is. I'll do a dry run, if you'll excuse the expression." He hopped bravely out in the weather and tried to get the thing unfurled. The wind kicked up again and almost blew him over, the tent flapping in the bushes.

After a while he came back to sit beside me, panting. "What an antique."

"You don't know how to put it up?" My teeth were chattering so I could hardly speak.

"At least I'm trying. You lug along a tent you expect others to put up for you!"

"You want me to help?"

"If it wouldn't be too much trouble."

I ignored his sarcasm and got out there, too, cold and wet as it was. While he hammered in the tent pegs I held the pole in place, barely. But he no sooner secured one side of the tent than the other flopped up again. "Find me some stones, quick!"

Awfully bossy, but I didn't argue. He knew more than I did about putting up tents in the teeth of a monsoon.

Finally we got it up and were inside. Phillip pitched the pack to the other end and zipped up the curtain. He took off his boots, the binoculars draped around his neck, and other knickknacks hanging on his belt. "See if your sleeping bag is dry and get out of those wet clothes."

I'll tell you, there's not much room to

maneuver in a backpacking tent, especially when you're stiff and cold. It took me a
while, but I pulled off my boots, got out my
rather dampish sleeping bag, and fluffed
it over me while I tried to pry the icy jeans
from my legs. Phillip lay down beside me,
turned in the other direction. At last I
gave up and lay back. Those jeans weren't
coming off until they dried, like some time
next week.

He turned back to me. His cheeks were
as red as his bandanna, brown curls bounc-
ing. He was a very alive-looking person,
I had to admit. "Haven't you got your wet
jeans off?"

"Look, I appreciate all you've done, but
come on. My pants are my business."

"You don't understand. It's very dangerous to get wet and cold up here."

"Hey, leave me alone! I'll take care of
it!"

"Better rub those legs, too," he ordered,
facing the other way again as I struggled
out of my jeans. "Get the circulation
going."

"When did you get your sergeant's
stripes?"

"I mean it, Bennet. If you don't, I'll have
to."

Have to, implying it would be a loathsome chore. Bossy, overbearing, a real Sea

Cliffie. Wait until we got back with the others. I would really tell him off then! I pulled on a pair of dry stirrup tights. But fair's fair. I handed him the pad I'd put under my bag the night before. "Here, you take this."

"No, I'll wrap up in my poncho. Thanks anyway. How about some gorp?"

I found it in my pack. We lay listening to the rain, if anything, coming down harder than ever. A real typhoon of a rain. I wondered what he was thinking about. Being the hero, finding the lost lamb? About how we would be teased tomorrow, for spending the night together? Or was he thinking of Libby Lou?

What I thought about was home. My own room, ah, I really love that room. In my mind I walked all around it, sitting down on the edge of my brass bed, my grandmother's quilt on it, red and pink and green. I stretched out on that soft, warm bed, turned up the controls on my mint-green electric blanket. . . .

A huge, pointed rock was drilling up between my shoulder blades, even through the pad. I just couldn't get warm. At last I said, "I wonder what they're doing up at the lake. Poor Mr. Quillan." I had a sudden thought. "He's going to be mad at you, too, Phil. You shouldn't have left without permission."

"Now you tell me." Phillip didn't sound sleepy, either.

"He'll be so glad to see both of us he won't say much," I decided.

"Maybe," Phillip didn't sound that sure. "You better eat some of this, too. It'll help keep you warm."

I took a handful of gorp and ate it slowly. He was silent again. I decided he *was* thinking about Libby Lou. A super-gust of wind almost lifted the tent from its anchors. "Too bad Libby Lou had to miss the trip," I said, and then I began laughing so hard I choked and wheezed.

He looked over alarmed, probably thinking I was having some kind of seizure. "What's going on with you?"

"Did you hear me? Actually pitying Libby Lou for having enough sense to stay in the dry, beautiful, safe, warm city!"

In the dusky light of the tent I could see him grin. "She was right about not wanting to come. It wouldn't have done for her."

"It's not doing for me, either," I said earnestly, fervently. "I've hated and loathed every minute so far, even before I got lost. I've never been so scared in my life." Then I remembered something.

"Phillip, I didn't tell you! There are bears around here. A huge bear and her cub — they stepped right out on the trail. They weren't black bears, either, the kind Mr. Quillan told us about."

He sat up at once. "Bears? You saw a bear?"

"And her cub. They were brown, though."

'Those *are* the black bears. I mean, they can be brown, too. What happened?"

"I played dead, curled up on the ground."

"Hey, that was a gutsy thing to do." I could hear the surprise in his voice.

"It was horrible, horrible. After about a thousand years they went away." I shuddered, remembering. "And I ran up the mountain. I told you I didn't leave the trail just for the fun of it!"

"I don't suppose they'd try anything in this storm but we better not chance it." He reached for my pack, dug out the cooking pot, tin cup, and plate I was carrying. "We'll use these for noise — bear bangers. And we'll have to take turns keeping watch."

"What do we do?"

"Simple. If we hear a sound we start slamming these babies together and yelling like crazy. Okay? I'll stand guard first."

I lay back down, not exactly relaxed. But I must have drifted off because Phillip was shaking my shoulder. "Okay, you're on. . . ."

He curled up in his poncho and I sat yawning in my sleeping bag, still cold. The wind had stopped, but the rain kept up an even pounding. It was black, black outside and morning was a million miles away. Finally Phillip took the bear bangers from me, and I stretched out again.

After a while I was aware of being warm and comfortable at last. When I awoke the rain had stopped, the sun was shining through the side of the tent, and I was snuggled next to Phillip.

Chapter 7

When I moved, Phillip rolled over, and then he opened his eyes. Talk about your double takes. He turned bright red and sat up as if he'd discovered a diamond-backed rattler in the tent.

"I thought you were standing guard, Phillip," I said as nastily as I could. "The bears, remember?"

"The last I remember you were on watch." He crawled out of the tent. "It doesn't matter. We're alive and well."

"And only minutes from the trail. Minutes!" I called. Who could be miffed about anything with that in mind?

There wasn't any answer. My heart stopped. Don't be an idiot, I said to myself. He's right out there. He wouldn't go off and leave you, he wasn't *that* revolted by you. I hid my relief when I heard his voice again.

"Okay, Bennet. Let's strike this antique and get back."

"Be right out." I ignored the slam to Ken's tent, rolled my wet jeans, put them in the pack and handed it out to him. "Give me a sec and I'm with you." It was my turn to retire to the bushes. Sun, wonderful warm sun, was shining down like the first day of creation. There was a smell of vanilla coming from the bark of a giant pine tree overhead.

Phillip had retied his red bandanna around his springy curls and swung into action. He had the tent down already. "I draped your jeans on the outside of the pack, see. They'll dry fast in the sun. We better have something to eat before we take off." He handed me my bag of cracker bread, cheddar cheese, candy, and figs. "This is all I could find."

"That's all there is." I sat down on the log beside him.

"For five days? Are you a bird or something? I could take care of all that right now."

"Be my guest."

"No, let's just eat a little." He put the lunches back in the pack. "To be super-super-safe, we should keep the rest of the food in reserve."

"Whatever you say." I smiled at him,

feeling very high and happy "At least the bears didn't attack last night."

"No thanks to the way we stood guard," he said, "but I guess you really needed to sack out."

Those green eyes looked me over curiously.

I turned away, hoping I wasn't blushing. "You were sleeping, too! Don't blame it on me!"

"I wasn't!" He swung the pack on his shoulders, my wet jeans dangling. "Why do you distort everything I say?"

"I don't distort everything you say! If you weren't so stuck on yourself you'd realize that."

"Stuck on myself? Where did that come from? What's with you this morning? Let's go. I want to deliver you back to Quillan, girl, and fast."

"Fine. Great! You don't know how much that suits me!"

He started off; I rushed along behind. I shouldn't be so mad at him, I told myself. He *had* found me. What would I have done last night without him? Someone had to put that tent up for me. I might not even be alive this morning if he hadn't come along, even if he wasn't as smart as he thought he was.

Phillip started off one way; then he changed directions.

My heart almost stopped. "Don't you know the way?"

"Of course I know the way! I came through here, picking up your things." But he looked around uncertainly.

I couldn't stand it. "If you'd left them there we would have had the way back marked!"

We glared at each other. Phillip turned away and started off again, and I trailed along behind, too crushed to cry.

We came out around a high granite mound, a boulder I seemed to remember, a gleaming mountain all by itself.

Phillip gave a yelp. "Yes! This *is* the way. I came right through there, see that twisted tree? See that?"

"Aww-right!" I was so relieved it was all I could do not to hug him.

"And the trail's right across — oh, no!"

"What *is* this?" It looked like the Mississippi in front of us. Yards wide and foaming. Talk about whitecaps — the water was plunging and boiling down a vast gorge, snagging off huge chunks of the bank as we watched.

"Where's that little creek, the one we crossed?" I bellowed over the noise of the river.

Phillip yelled back, "This *is* the little creek! All that rain last night," I could see he was shaken.

"We can't possibly get across!"

He shook his head. "Not a chance. But we'll go find a place where we *can* cross." Up ahead on our side of the river was an enormous cliff; downstream it was less impossible, but there were terrible boulders we would have to climb over. My heart sank even lower.

It was just plain terrifying, having to step out on slippery granite with nothing but my boots to hold me. "Put your feet down hard!" Phillip called over his shoulder. "You get traction that way. Don't pussyfoot!"

Bossy! Bossy! But he was a pro out here and I was a real drag, I realized. We had gone about fifty yards, and I couldn't help noticing the stream looked as wild and uncrossable as ever.

"Don't worry," Phillip shouted. "Once we find a good place to cross, we'll just follow the stream up the other side. No problem! I have an excellent compass." He patted one of the little cases hanging from his belt.

It was nice of him to explain, when I had been kind of mouthy earlier. "Thank you,

Phillip. I can tell you've done this a lot. And who knows why," I added under my breath.

"Actually, I haven't. Only once, in fact. My father took me when I was about ten years old."

"What happened? Didn't you like it?"

"I liked it fine. I really loved it. But it was a bad scene for my father. I really messed up that trip."

"How come you messed up?" I wanted to keep him talking for a minute, I needed a little breather. An absolutely giant boulder was up ahead.

"I just didn't play it smart. I got about a million blisters, and I could barely walk after the first day. I lost my camera in the creek." He looked now like he was sorry he'd started remembering. "The crusher was that I couldn't seem to catch on to fishing. My father spent most of the trip untangling my line from bushes and trees. Poor Dad."

"Why not poor little Phillip?"

He grinned again. I must say he had incredible teeth, some of the best I've seen around, very white in his tan face. "Actually, that's what I thought, at the time. But I can see how it was — a macho outdoorsman, and here's this wimpy kid."

"You never got to go again?"

"My mother and dad got divorced that winter and he moved to New York."

"If you only went that once, how come you know these things, about the bears and all?"

"I listened to what Quack Quillan told us, which obviously you didn't bother to do. And I read a lot about backpacking. When this trip came up, I knew it was for me." His face darkened. "Which caused trouble with Libby Lou."

"Well, don't expect sympathy from me. I'm on her side on this. Not that I'm interested."

"Listen, why did you say I was stuck on myself? What did you mean by that crack?"

"Oh, well. Couldn't we have a little gorp before we go on?" I took it out of the pack pocket. "Here, finish it off. It's just an impression my friend Darcie and I got the other day. A couple of weeks ago in Golden Gate Park? We said hello and you just blasted by us without a word."

"So that was it. Bennet," he looked me seriously in the face. "I don't remember doing that. I mean, I remember that day, I'd just had a fight with Libby Lou. We'd gone down to see her mother, she volunteers at the museum, and Libby Lou needed some money. But then she announces that not only is she not going on this trip, but I shouldn't go, either, and — well, I saw red. I didn't even see you!"

"Do you often have such fights with her that you don't know what you're doing afterward?"

"Not often." He grinned suddenly. "And we always make up. That's kind of nice."

"I'm sure it is," I said stiffly, hating him for having memories like that. "Look, the sun's almost to the middle of the sky. If we don't get there pretty soon, we'll miss them going back down for help. We've got to get on that trail!"

"Right." Phillip started scaling the granite mountain in front of us, and I fell in behind him. "This will be a piece of cake," he said.

It was horrible.

"Put your left boot up there, Bennet. By that root, see, and then your right hand in this crack here — you can do it."

"If I don't look down, that is." I didn't dare look up, either. "Personally, I think this is very, very dangerous."

"What else can we do? If we start trying to circle around all this stuff we'll really be in trouble. It's easy to get confused out here without a map. One more, there — let me give you a hand." Finally we were on top.

From there we could see the stream had split into four streams.

"Aww-right!" Phillip yelled. "We can cross these babies one at a time. Come on, it'll be a lot easier going down the other side of this thing."

I followed him down, but I was beginning to have terrible doubts.

Did he really know what he was doing?

We crossed the second split-off stream on more big rocks. The ground on the other side was very mushy. Our boots stuck at each step as we floundered along. There weren't any rocks in the next branch.

"We can wade this one." Phillip sat down, stripped off his boots, rolled up his jeans, stuffed his socks inside his boots, tied them together by the laces, and draped them around his neck. I clenched my teeth and did the same, pushing my tights up above my knees. Clouds were coming up, I noticed, and I prayed they weren't rain clouds.

"Oh! *Ohhh*." I had expected the water to be cold, but it was so icy I was surprised I didn't drop dead from the shock. As it was, my heart did a complete flip-flop. My poor heart. It had had a workout these last couple of days.

I took a deep breath and plowed through the icy water after Phillip. From the knees down I felt like I was being crushed to ice cubes on the sharp, slick rocks. When we scrambled up the bank on the other side our feet were splotched purple, and no wonder.

"Wow! We better get our boots on fast. It's very important not to get cold out here, Bennet. You let yourself get wet and cold, and it can be lights out." He took a quick look at the sky. The clouds were boiling up again.

We squished on for a long time. It seemed to me the stream was looping around a lot. At last it spread out into a big pond in front of us. "Hey, Phillip. Now we can't even see the other streams!"

"Yeah, I know. They really separate sometimes. But as long as we're heading due east we're okay. I'll just check that again." He reached for the compass case on his belt — and stopped dead.

"Phillip, what is it?"

He didn't look at me. "The compass. It's not in there."

What was there to say?

"I don't believe this! It must have come open and fallen out going through that brush. Or crossing the stream." He turned a white, miserable face to me. "How could I have been so stupid?"

"Hey, it's not your fault. Everyone loses things. It's my fault, too; I should have kept an eye on it."

"Looked after me? I'm such a klutz I can't manage to hang on to my compass by myself!" His voice was tight with misery.

"That's a really dumb way to look at it."

"That's how my father would have looked at it." He sat down heavily on a log. "This would be no more than he would have expected."

"Well, he'd be wrong! And we don't need a compass, really. We'll just follow the stream." Except now it was a pond. My voice faltered, but I went on, "We'll go around this pond and — you *do* know where the trail is." The sky was almost black, as if in response to the way I was feeling.

"Yeah. Sure." He got up. "We better mush on."

I knew how low he was feeling. "Stop blaming yourself. Forget your father. How could he know what we're up against here?" All the time I was speaking I was aware of the panic welling up inside me. I spoke quickly to keep ahead of it. "Besides, they're out looking for us by now. Mr. Quillan is back at the trailhead, I bet, and they've called the rangers and everybody." Including my mother. My throat tightened, but I continued, "Pretty soon we'll hear them, or better yet, see them coming."

"Hey, shut up, will you?" he said quietly. "I don't need you to jolly me along as if I were a scared, little boy."

"Don't tell me to shut up! If you're not a scared little boy, why act like one? Just because you lost an old compass."

He swung around and glared at me. "You don't know enough to realize what this means, do you?" His voice got louder. "Slowing down the whole trip — spearing me with a fork — why did I think I had to come back to find you?" What mean green eyes he had! "If you weren't such an airhead, you wouldn't have lost the trail in the first place!"

"You didn't have to come back for me! But you wanted to play the big hero, didn't you? Stuck-up snob!" My face was boiling with rage. It had struck me full force. Phillip Hargrove wasn't going to be able to get us back! He didn't know the way any more than I did!

"You're really something." He kept glaring down at me. "Talk about gratitude.

Well, let me tell you something, Bennet Kinnell: It's going to be the high point of my life when I get you off my hands."

"I'm not *on* your hands!" I screamed, beyond myself by now. "You don't have to stay with me!"

Phillip stood up, his eyes shooting sparks at me.

"Go, go!" I couldn't stop. "Not that you'll know which way, since you were stupid enough to lose the compass!"

A terrible, familiar crack of thunder almost drowned out my words. "Go! What are you waiting for?" My heart stopped dead in its tracks. He couldn't go off and leave me alone again! But I heard my crazy voice going on, "You take half of the food — "

"Why not the tent, too, since you'd never get it up alone in a million years!" He dug furiously in the pack. "Here, get these on. Do I have to tell you it's raining?" He handed me my rain gear, and struggled into his big blue poncho. The rain was hitting the leaves with an ominous rattle.

After a while I said as coolly as I could, "We're going to stay together, then?" The raindrops were making big, sad circles on the pond.

"We're stuck with each other until somebody finds us. And I want you to know

I don't like it any better than you do. Okay?"

"Okay." I wiped away the tears streaking my cheeks, hoping he thought it was the rain.

Chapter 8

"Well, we can't stand here," Phillip said irritably, yanking his poncho over the pack. "We've got to find higher ground."

We stumbled up from the pond and found ourselves under some trees against a cliff.

It came to me that it would have been smart to mark the way we had come this morning so we could go back if we couldn't get across the stream or — as it had turned out — streams. He should have thought of that! I had to face it; I couldn't rely on him.

It gets very boring, staring out at rain. My thoughts got bleaker and bleaker. I realized that I was starving. "I think we should have something to eat."

"We don't have much *to* eat." Phillip sounded more down than I was. Because he was stuck with me, no doubt. "Except oatmeal, we've got enough of that to last all summer, and the way things are going — "

"Phillip! How about we make a fire and cook some of it? We've got that pot. We could get dry from the fire, too."

"What are we going to burn?" We both looked out at the water running over the dripping bushes in front of us.

A warm, cheery, leaping fire. I wanted that almost as much as I wanted some hot food and a soft place to sit down, and most of all to see the searchers coming through the trees.

"Wait a minute." Phillip crawled further back in the boulders. "There might be some dry stuff under these low branches — Hey, hey, hey!"

I squirmed back to where he was. It was more protected by the cliff overhang back there, and he had found two dry little sticks."

"You do have matches?"

"Do I have matches." He reached in his pocket and brought out a flat tin box wrapped in oiled cloth. "I only hope your matches match up to these." He put about a dozen on the ledge and rewrapped the box before slipping it in his pocket again.

Naturally I didn't mention my non-existent matches.

"Maybe I can find enough wood for a fire

in other places like this. I'll go look." He plunged out in the storm.

I sat miserably aware of the dampness inside my jacket. Suppose he didn't come back? Of course he was coming back! Unless he got lost — a distinct possibility, considering his record so far. I made myself study the leaves pasted on the stone in front of me. Narrow, oval leaves with jagged edges, a glossy beige against black-and-white rock. Suppose he met a bear. Those same bears, following us. I told myself to notice how great nature is at putting things together: polished beige leaves, the rough salt-and-pepper stone. I wiped my forehead. Or how about the shape of that raindrop, stretching out to a narrow-waisted streak before it was a splash of crystal on the stone? I would sit here and he would never come back. His mauled body would stay out there. . . .

A full year passed before I heard him coming.

He was carrying dry-looking branches; his blue poncho swung out happily as he scrambled up the rocks. "Good news!"

"They've found us!" I leaped over the bushes to meet him, happiness pouring over me in huge, glorious waves. "They've come!"

"No, hey, no!" he said quickly. "But I've found us a great place, higher up on this cliff. A real cave loaded with dry wood! But I've got some bad news, too."

I sank back under the sheltering rock, numb with disappointment. "Bears?" I managed to say calmly after a pause. Inside me a little person had flung herself down in a storm of screaming and weeping. "I wouldn't want to take over any bear's cave."

"No chance of that. They're not hibernating this late. They're up and around."

"That has to be your bad news?"

"I wish it were. I've lost the rest of the matches. They must have slipped out when I was getting water, but I can't see them down there. At least we have these." He picked up the matches on the ledge, carefully wrapped them in plastic and put them deep in the pack.

I leaped to my feet. "A warm, dry place — let's go!"

"Oh, no! We can't go in the cave during this kind of cloudburst."

I actually hopped up and down with rage. "Are you crazy? We're drowning out here! What is wrong with your head?"

"No, no." He said impatiently. "I read that a cave is the most dangerous place during an electrical storm. It draws the lightning. We're a lot safer here, under a lot of low trees."

"Then why tell me about it? That's the meanest — "

He got mad, too. "Because when it stops thundering and carrying on we can go in! I brought back wood for a fire here."

"You'll never be able to get one started," I said bitterly. The little person inside me was wailing like a hound dog.

Ignoring me, he hunched over and carefully built a tiny pyramid. Dry leaves first, then the smallest twigs and so on, working up to a thin branch. "Bennet," he glanced up at me, and just for the moment I forgot how gross a personality he had and thought how Darcie would have drooled. Shadows molded his strong, high cheekbones, making his green eyes greener, somehow. Glossy brown hair, the red bandanna; I found myself wishing he would smile so I could get the white teeth, too, the whole picture. "You wouldn't have any paper in your pack, would you?"

"Don't go away." I crawled over to the pack, and pulled out a sopping roll of toilet paper and then a handful of mushy glop that was once a packet of tissues. "I guess I should have put them in plastic bags?"

He nodded grimly. My cheeks flamed, but

then I remembered. "Hold on. I brought a book," I fished out my paperback, and sure enough, the center pages were dry. "Here, tear out some pages from the middle."

Phillip glanced at the cover. *New Directions in Textiles.* "You know, you are one weird girl."

"What's so strange about wanting to learn about fabrics? I'm going to be a textile artist."

"How about that." Very, very slowly he struck a match and put it to the page he'd shredded. Nothing. But two matches later a beautiful little flame flickered; he blew at it delicately. I held my breath. More leaves and twigs caught, and already I could feel the gorgeous warmth of it. I took my jeans, wetter than ever, from the pack and spread them on the rocks above the fire.

Phillip got to his feet. "Where's the pot? How much water do you need to cook oatmeal?"

"You cook it with water?"

"Of course you cook it with water! How could you not know that!" He gave me a black look and crawled out. I heard his boots clanking on the granite.

All right, I felt like a fool. But was it my fault my mother never let me do any cooking? My only experience with oatmeal had been sitting down in front of a steaming hot bowl of it. With fat, brown raisins and creamy milk. Hot chocolate in my Bavarian mug. I swallowed sadly and untied the oatmeal bag, and found a little paper folded on the top. Aha, a formula of some kind, and me practically a mathematical whiz. . . .

When Phillip came back in with the pot of water, I said briskly, "Pour all that out except two cups. That'll make four servings; we can each eat two, can't we? When the water boils we add this much oatmeal, stir, wait a minute, and that's it."

"You're a quick learner, I'll say that." He looked at me suspiciously. "Or," he reached for a tiny bottle of water purification tablets in his shirt pocket, "were you putting me on?"

"Would I do that? If you must know, there are directions here for cooking oatmeal for twenty-five people, and if I do say it myself, I'm a killer math student."

"Rah-rah for you."

Let him be sarcastic; I didn't care. We were going to have something hot to eat! While we were waiting for the water to purify, inspiration struck me. I dug out my lunch. I carefully tore two of the figs into tiny bits and stirred them into the dry oatmeal.

Phillip made a prop for the pot with three of the bigger branches; he set it carefully over the flames. We watched as if it were filled with diamonds. He fed wood under it and, at last, at last it boiled. We tossed in the oatmeal, stirred, and waited.

I gave him my spoon, I took the fork, and we both ate out of the pot.

"I don't think I've ever tasted anything this good before. I'm beginning to feel human," he said, smiling.

I grinned back. "I actually think the rain is slacking off out there, too." I felt so good I added, "I'm surprised we don't hear them looking for us. They can look in the rain, can't they?"

"I don't know. Listen, Bennet. I don't know how to say it, but this is important." He paused uncertainly, and just for a second, I felt sorry for him. "I know how you feel about me, okay? As a matter of fact, you're not my type, either, even before I knew about your personality."

I began to bristle but he looked me full in the face, and the most indescribable feeling swept over me. "But we've got to forget this personal stuff."

"What personal stuff?" I said huskily, wishing he hadn't felt he had to come right out and tell me how unattractive he thought I was. "Get to the point."

"The point is we've got to stop fighting and start cooperating. If we're going to get out of this alive."

My heart lurched to a stop. "Of course we're getting out of this alive! They're searching for us right now, I know they are! In a few hours — "

"I hope so. I sure hope so. I know they'll start searching as soon as they can. But these flooded streams are no easier for them to cross than for us. How can they see anything from the air, with this rain? No, it's up to us. We've got to use our heads, and make sure we survive until they can find us."

Both of us together. I couldn't keep putting it all on him. He didn't know much more about staying alive out here than I did.

"Well, I can overlook your personality if you can put up with mine until we're home safe and sound." With your precious, stuck-up Libby Lou, I felt like adding.

"Okay. Let's declare peace and work together on this thing. Separating would be suicide for both of us. No matter how much it bothers you, you've got to stick with me."

"I can see that." Obviously it bothered him a whole lot to be stuck with me.

"It's our best shot." He kept looking

earnestly into my face. "I remember reading once about the Korean War, in the fifties? Conditions in the prison camps were really gross. The Americans dropped like flies, dying off at a terrible rate. But the Turkish prisoners — it was a United Nations army, sort of — nearly all survived. Know why?"

"They had better relations with the Koreans or something?" I was very glad we were having this talk. We had to be on the same side, and get a working relationship going.

"No way. All the prisoners were treated the same way by the enemy. Rotten. But the Turkish prisoners took care of each other. They shared what food they had. If someone got sick, they took turns nursing him back to health. They had a real kind of brotherhood going there, and it saved their lives."

"Okay, you've made your point. We put our feelings aside, we don't make personal remarks or cut each other down. I won't even mention Libby Lou's name."

"I'd appreciate it. You and I are partners until we're found. Shake?"

I reached over for his hand, thinking he probably wouldn't notice I have rather nice hands, small and slim. "Kinnell and Hargrove, till death — oh, I don't mean that, erase, erase — until the *searchers* do us part."

He didn't even smile. "We've got to sharpen up, from now on. No more losing stuff."

"About the compass," I said, licking my fork. "I'm sorry I blew all that off about you being stupid. I'm no one to talk. I better tell you. I didn't bring any matches, like Mr. Quillan said."

"Didn't bring any matches!" But he stopped himself. "Okay, that's good. I mean, that you told me. We've got to know what we have to deal with. These are all the matches, then. We'll have to be careful with them." He sighed, and then looked straight at me with those remarkable green eyes. "I better confess to you. I've lost my binoculars, too. Compass, matches, *and* binocs. Even my father wouldn't expect that. I left them hanging on a tree back there where we camped." He rubbed his chin grimly.

"Oh," I said. "Oh, well. That's the breaks. We'll manage."

He started digging in the pack. "Let's check out the food, make sure just how much, or how little, I should say, we have."

We looked it over. The gorp was gone, and there were only three pieces of cracker bread left — I'd figured a slice a day — five figs, a bag of lemon drops, and a square of cheddar cheese. When I thought of the extra food Dee had offered me that I had been too lazy to carry — well, there was no point in bringing that up. "Wait a minute. What's this?" There was a flat foil package at the bottom of my food bag I hadn't seen before. "I didn't pack that!" I unwrapped one of those big, solid chocolate bars. Around it was a little note. "Tuck this in your sleeping bag tonight, honey. Don't forget the teeth! Love, Mom."

"Isn't that sweet! She knows how much I love chocolate."

"She doesn't know much about bears, though. You tuck that in your sleeping bag and you might be unpleasantly surprised. Anything else in there?"

That was it.

"We won't starve," I pointed out. "We can always make a fire and cook oatmeal. There's loads and loads, we can't possibly run out of that before they find us."

"We're quite a way from the trail now." Phil bent over to feed the last little branches into the fire, and I couldn't see his face.

"They could find us here! A plane will spot us! A helicopter." But would it, I wondered. All these trees. . . .

"Maybe. The thing is, without the compass, and the way the stream has split up and turned into ponds and looped around this crazy way, I don't think we could ever get across all of it, and go back up the other side, like I thought. That's not going to work."

"Now you tell me!" I took a deep breath, and fought to get my anger, panic really, under control. I wiped my fork clean with some of the mushy tissue. "Sorry, I didn't mean to yell. Then I think we should go back to where we were. Back to where you *know* where the trail is, even if there is a river between **us** and it. The rain can't last forever. It's got to go back down to a creek sometime."

"I agree, absolutely. But," he licked the last of the oatmeal out of the pot with his fingers. "Problem — partner. The rain is making the stream we waded higher by the minute. Also, the one we crossed on the rocks? We may not be able to get back across them for a while."

"Okay. We'll wait it out here."

"We don't have any choice." He paused and I could see he was really depressed. "Without the compass, and streams going off everywhere, how could we find the way we came? We'd go around in circles. More circles," he corrected himself bitterly.

The rain ran coldly down inside my collar. I heard the mournful trickling of water on the granite outside.

Phillip had gotten us more lost than ever. No wonder his father thought he was a prize klutz in the woods. The knot in my stomach tightened. He wasn't any better at this than I was. There was no one out here to take care of little Bennet — except me.

I looked down at the chocolate bar still in my hand and thought of my mother putting it there. By now, probably, she knew I was lost. I clenched my teeth and fought back terrible sobs.

After a while I was able to say in a strangled voice, "What you're saying is, we're way worse off than we were yesterday?"

He nodded miserably. "We should have stayed right there where I found you and waited for them. I *knew* that. All the books say that. But with the trail so close — "

I looked up at the piece of sky visible between the boulder and cliff. Dark, pouring, endless rain. A disgusting sob escaped me.

"It's okay, Bennet. Go ahead and cry if it'll make you feel any better. I don't blame you for being scared."

"I'm not scared! It's my mother. By now

she'll know and she'll just die. Won't yours?"

"I suppose so. But Gerald, that's my stepfather, he's good at calming people down." He shoved the oatmeal pot out in the rain to rinse. "By now they've probably called my dad in New York. And he's wondering why they let an idiot like me go to the mountains again." He added gloomily, "I hope they aren't fighting about it."

To get his mind off that, I said, "I thought maybe your father was dead, like mine. I'm glad he's alive, even if he doesn't live with you anymore."

"I'm sorry yours is dead," he said listlessly.

"That's okay. I don't remember him at all, hardly." I checked my jeans plastered on the rock. Wetter than ever. "Maybe my mom wouldn't be so jumpy if he were alive. She's such a worrier. If I'm five minutes late getting home — she was terrified about this trip in the first place. I'm sure she never expected me to survive it. And now...." My voice trailed off.

"She doesn't need to worry. I'll tell her myself when we get back. You may look kind of delicate, but you're one tough hombre, Bennet Kinnell." He flashed those perfect, white teeth.

"Thanks a lot." Much as it cheered me

to hear him speak of us getting back, I didn't especially care to be called a tough hombre. But that's what I'd have to be, until we got back. "I thought we were going to knock off the personal remarks?"

"I meant that as a compliment. I meant — oh, forget it. Sorry, sorry." He unfolded his legs and managed to stand up, more or less. "The wind has really died down. There hasn't been any thunder for an hour or so. Would it be safe to go to the cave? We've both got to decide."

I tried to think as clearly as I could. It seemed to me the rain had let up, too. "Let's go. We could die of the cold if we don't get out of this wet. I know! Let's take some of this fire in the pot so we won't have to use up anymore matches."

"That is a truly spectacular idea." He gave me a look that made me glow, cold as I was.

We used the spoon and fork to put some of the best coals on a bed of sand in the pot, and kicked sand over what was left of the fire.

"Don't you think it's getting light over that way?" I asked as we clattered down the granite. I had my permanently wet jeans over my arm and carried the pot with the coals. Phil had the pack. "Maybe the rain will be over soon, too."

"Let's hope. Bennet, I've just thought of something! When it clears we could get our directions again from the sun. But the problem, since we are backtracking, would be to keep going due west . . . no, we better stay here," he said, as if talking to himself, as we scrambled up the rocks to the cave.

"Now, *this* is what I call all right!" I told him. It was dry, and for a cave, spacious. I could almost stand upright. It was, in fact, about the size of a good closet, the walk-in kind. I tried not to think of my own dear closet. My school skirts hanging in a neat plaid row next to jeans and pants, the sweaters in their plastic bags on the shelves. The jackets. My shoes on the racks. It just didn't seem possible that someone with such a well-organized, *civilized* closet could be out here, blundering around in a cold rain. I tried to switch off my mood by congratulating Phil again on finding this terrific cave.

After we got the fire going, he rigged up a rack for my jeans and our damp rainwear. I got out the rolled-up sleeping bag and pad, and we leaned on them, almost at ease.

The rain kept right on falling outside, but now it was a peaceful kind of rain.

"I don't think much is going to happen

today," he said after a while, regretfully.
I almost didn't hear. I was getting sleepy
from the warmth and dryness, a fabulous
combination of feelings I had never appre-
ciated before. "I'll take the tent rope and
hang the food up in a tree before it gets
dark. You want something more to eat
first?"

"Let's have some of the chocolate." I
broke off two small pieces and ate mine as
slowly as I could. I know Phillip, like me,
wanted to wolf it all down, but we put it
in the bag with the rest of the food.

"Tomorrow will be another day, partner," I said, putting on my rain jacket and
pants; I had to learn how to keep the food
safe. "They'll find us for sure. And we'll
manage until they do. No more bickering."
I spoke as cheerfully as I could, to wall off
the way I felt, seeing darkness coming
again. Darkness in the wilderness is such
black, overpowering darkness. But surely
they would find us tomorrow!

"Tomorrow for sure," he answered
heartily. "We're going to be okay, now
that we're working together. Even if we
don't care that much for each other." He
turned to steady me down a rather nasty
ledge. "You can't help how you feel about
people, can you? Chemistry, I guess. I remember when I saw Libby Lou, after she

came back from being in England for a year — " he stopped abruptly.

"If you don't mind I'd rather not hear about your great romance," I said sharply.

"Don't worry, you won't. You don't really like her, do you?" He swung around, the bag of food clutched against his blue poncho, as if he found this amazing. His eyelashes were spiky with rain.

"We don't spend a lot of time together, you may have noticed. She's all right, I guess. But I'm not the one in love with her." I should have stopped right there, but my smart mouth had to add, "and that *dah*ling British accent."

"You don't play fair, Bennet." He stomped angrily along in front of me and didn't say another word. I watched him tie a rock to one end of the rope and swing it, first try, over a high branch.

By the time the food was hanging safely in the tree, the silence between us was very heavy. It was far too late to say I was sorry.

Silently we returned to the cave. Silently he put more wood on the fire.

And silently I took off my boots and got into the sleeping bag. The pad I laid out for him; it was only fair. The ground was hard and cold.

That's all I remember until I awoke in the dark, and for a wonderful, sweet second, I thought I was home. The fire had gone out and I had rolled over against Phillip.

I pulled myself back in a hurry. I sat staring down through the darkness at him, listening to his steady breathing. Outside there was nothing but a totally frightening silence broken only by the usual sound of rain.

The rain would never stop. The streams we were caught in would turn into one big lake. We would have to stay up on the granite, in this cave forever.

All that darkness outside, miles and miles of nothing but dark, wet trees and black skies. And us at the bottom of it, now more lost than ever. We could have been on a different planet. Two nights, and we were still cut off from our real lives. My mother. Darcie. What would they think of me out here, for the first time in my life on my own? Would I ever see them again? The knot in my stomach pulled tighter.

I couldn't help it. I hitched my bag nearer to Phillip. I needed to be close to him. It didn't matter that he didn't like me and I didn't really like him. I imagined I could hear the faint *chunk-chunk* of his heart. His shirt smelled of woodsmoke. This boy who wasn't and never would be for me.

I matched my breathing to his, and had drifted off to sleep when it happened.

Craa-ck! Like the sound of a gun going off outside.

We leaped up so fast we cracked our heads together.

Chapter 9

Phil rushed to the entrance of the cave. He hopped back at once to pull on his boots. "Can't see anything. You wait here."

But I grabbed my boots, too, and caught up with him a few yards down the granite.

"Our food! That crack was the branch breaking!" he called.

By now I could see the bear at the base of the tree about thirty feet away. Rooting in our food bag!

Everything dipped and began to go black. I grabbed for Phil's arm.

He shook me off and kept sliding down. "It can't take our food!"

I slid right behind him. "It'll attack us!"

"I'll scare it away. Hey, go back for the pots to bang."

I charged back up for the pot and cup. By the time I got to Phil, he was slowly approaching the bear. It was huge and it looked at us menacingly.

"Phil, come back! Let's hide in the cave. What's a little food? Please, Phil!"

He grabbed up a good-sized rock and heaved it near the bear. "Bang those pots. Bang them!"

My hands were shaking, but I clattered and banged. So did my heart.

The bear took a step toward us. I could see dirty-yellow, pointy fangs. Phil bellowed and threw another rock.

The bear stopped and looked thoughtful. Phil waved his arms and yelled louder. I pounded harder on the pots, trying to shout, too, but my throat had closed.

With a last look at the mess it had made, the bear turned and lumbered away into the woods.

"Quick!" Phil dashed over and scooped up the shredded bag that had held our food. Oatmeal was scattered around like snow.

We took the bag back up to the cave. The bear had cleaned us out. Crackers, lemon drops, figs, cheese were gone without a trace. All that was left of the chocolate bar was mangled foil.

"Why didn't we eat it all last night," I moaned.

"It didn't get all of the oatmeal."

"We should have eaten that chocolate bar the minute we found it!" I was getting madder the more I thought of it. "We had only one tiny little square each!"

"I'd say about four cups are left. Why didn't I string up the food so the bear couldn't get it? Idiot, idiot, idiot! Feeble. Weak. First the matches, and now this!"

"My very favorite kind. My mother knows how I like the dark, semi-sweet — " I stopped, suddenly hearing what he was saying. "Four cups of oatmeal to last until they find us?"

"If we can keep it from the bears." Phil's eyes were glowing green with anger. "Quack Quillan told us about a way to counterbalance the food so there's no rope dangling for them to get. Why didn't I work that out last night?"

"In a driving rainstorm? Come on, Phil. You were outstanding to get the food hung up at all. I know now how hard that is."

"For all the good it did I shouldn't have bothered." I could tell he was thinking again about what his macho father would have said.

"It did a lot of good! The bear didn't get all of it. Four cups of oatmeal; that means we can have a cup a day for four days."

"We can't be sure they'll find us in four

days." He went out and hunched on a rock near the cave entrance, too down to start the fire.

"Phil! They'll find us long before that! And look. Have you noticed what's spectacularly different about today? The sun is shining. Drying up the streams! They'll find us today." Looking around at the sunshine glittering on the wet, silver pine needles, showing up even more white flowers in the mossy grass at the edge of the water, I was suddenly sure of it.

Phil gave me a lopsided smile. His face was pale except where it was smudged with ash, but there was still dynamite in that smile. "Okay, Bennet. Now that we're down to this cruddy oatmeal, I'll figure out a way to hang it so they don't get it, in case we are out here for another night. But I wish I'd stop making these dumb, stupid, costly mistakes."

"We hung the food together, remember? Anyway, there won't be any more goof-ups."

"Right. Nothing left for me to mess up."

"Phil! You're forgetting. We're in this together; you're not in charge."

He frowned; I hoped he got my point.

I went back to the cave and found my jeans were dry enough to wear. "Do you have water for the oatmeal?"

"In my canteen," he called. "I'm making the fire now. Bring some of your pages. We've got to do it with one match."

I brought my sleeping bag out to air, suddenly concerned with things I hadn't thought about the last couple of days. Like getting washed, brushing my teeth, changing my underwear and socks. Clean underwear! Even a clean shirt; I'd brought several. I told Phil my plans. "I've got soap, toothpaste, and an extra bandanna you can have for a towel. You could brush your teeth with a twig or something."

"The Indians used part of the soap plant for a toothbrush. Yeah, we might as well clean up while we wait for them. Look at all that water." The pond had extended itself ten yards toward us.

"They're sure to find us today," I assured him. "But just for the heck of it, let's mark which way is west, now that we can. With my back to the cave, west is right, toward that tree over there. I'll mark which tree." If it clouded over again and for some reason they didn't find us today, well, at least we would know our directions.

"Hey, that's good, Bennet!" He went with me over to the tree, looking down at me admiringly, I thought. "Smart thinking. Here, I'll carve it, W for west. Now that we know where west is, we could just keep lining up other trees with this one to sight on, as we go along. From here, it's a straight line to the dead tree there, see? That way we could keep on course, if we had to go back on our own. Thanks to you, partner, we'll lick this yet."

It gave me a warm, little feeling when he called me "partner." I said quickly, "They'll spot us today, anyway. But where could a helicopter land around here?"

"I've been thinking about that." He rubbed his handsome chin. "After breakfast let's climb to the top of this ridge behind us. We might even be able to see the trail from up there. We can check out a place for the helicopter to land. We may even see them looking for us."

In spite of the loss of our food, I was feeling better and better. "We'll mark our way up there, Phil. Let's make ducks, those stone piles, nonstop."

"You're really getting good at being lost! Absolutely no more going off without marking a trail." He gave me a very nice smile.

Hurriedly I measured out the oatmeal and stirred; we waited hungrily for it to thicken.

It doesn't take long to eat half a cup of oatmeal. It made me feel emptier than ever. We scraped the pot clean.

"Did I ever mention that I detest oatmeal, back in real life?" Phil said musingly. "Never touch the stuff. Take that glob on the rim, partner. It's yours."

But I knew he was at least as hungry as I was, so I put down my fork, wishing I didn't feel that little thrill when he called me partner.

"Floods. Bears. Holing up in caves. Hey, we could sell our story to the movies, *Adventures with Bennet and Phil*." He poured water in our scraped-clean pot. "Libby Lou will understand."

"I thought we weren't going to talk about personal matters," I reminded him. "Although I'd like to point out there's nothing *for* Libby Lou to understand."

"I know that," he said tersely. "What happens here in the woods has nothing to do with my relationship with her. That's different." He stopped. "Sorry. You don't want to hear about that."

"You're so right." I smiled sweetly at him. There was no way he could know how I was dying, *dying*, masochist that I was, to hear all about him going with that airhead.

He kept staring at me.

"What is it, Phil?"

He didn't answer. There was one of those total stillnesses, as if the world had stopped. My heart caught.

"You have the bluest eyes I've ever seen," he blurted out. "I mean, they're unreal."

For a moment neither one of us said anything. We listened to the water running over the rocks. A bird trilled a lot of sweet, flutey little notes. Shafts of morning sun slanted down through the high, dark-green pine branches like something in a Disney movie.

I broke the spell. "That's another thing. I better take my contacts out. It's been days." Why did I have to say that? I blundered on nervously. "Phil, you can tell me about Libby Lou if you want to. I'll listen, and I'll keep my mouth shut. After all, we're partners now. That's almost like being friends." Sometimes I really surprised myself, the things I came out with.

He kept looking at me. "I'm glad you call me Phil. No one else does. My mother, at school, everywhere. Phillip. Even," he hesitated, "even Libby Lou calls me Phillip."

"You don't care what *she* calls you." My mouth had a mind of its own.

"Of course not," he said soberly.

It served me right. I hoped he wouldn't want to talk about her anymore today.

We were both anxious to get to the top of the ridge, but Phil wanted to work out the bear-proof way of bagging food before we went.

"We could carry that little bit of oatmeal with us, you know," I pointed out.

"But I — *we* have got to rope it up safely at night," he explained. "It's a matter of balancing two bags without any ropes dangling. But then there has to be some way to get them down. . . . "

I could see he wanted to handle that problem, so I left him to it and took my clean clothes and the pot full of water up on a high, white boulder, well away from the pond. Mr. Quillan had made a big thing of not polluting streams. I kept an eye out for planes and helicopters, and tried not to think of food.

It was a gorgeous morning. Sunshine dazzled on everything. I noticed more and more flowers: lush, tall, orange ones like lilies, and delicate, little blue-purple bells. There were iridescent blue flashes over the pond; dragonflies, I decided. Lots of rich smells in the air, mild mint or sage, even an oniony whiff mixed in with the pine scent. The sun was getting higher; I could feel its heat on my arms.

It was sheer bliss, washing and putting on clean clothes. I decided to wash my hair, and went for yet another pot of water. In the clear pond I could see what appeared to to be my same old self: the blur of a clean blue shirt, a mop of tangled hair. I bent closer and studied my eyes. *You have the bluest eyes I've ever seen. Unreal.* He didn't say he liked them or anything, it was just a remark. People say things like that. Curiosities. A two-headed snake, the largest watermelon.

People say things all the time that are meaningless. I thought of the sudden silence after he'd said it. Was that meaningless, too? It didn't matter. Today for sure they'd find us. After today it wouldn't matter what he thought of me.

Phil washed up, too. He had figured out how to counterbalance two limp, little plastic bags of our oatmeal on a branch of the biggest tree around. "To get it down, we take this long stick I found, see that little notch on the end? With that we can get a grip on the knotted rope at the top. Is that neat or is that neat?"

"I just hope the bears haven't figured it out, too."

"We're a jump ahead of them this time. Okay, let's go."

We stopped every few yards and made little piles of stones, our own ducks. It took us a long time to get to the top of the ridge. My stomach growled with hunger. I knew Phil must be starving, too, but, silently, it had been agreed that we wouldn't talk about the fact that we couldn't eat again until tomorrow morning, or until we were found. Whichever came first.

The ridge was narrow on top, but wide enough for a helicopter to land, we decided. There was quite a bit of dirty-looking snow back under the twisted pine trees, and of course rocks, big and little, all over the place. A tawny animal, about the size of our cat Gullie but shaggier, darted under one of them.

"Marmot," Phil whispered. "They love sunning on the rocks." We could see the marmot's fat little face, watching us curiously from under a shelf of rock.

We looked in all directions, but we couldn't see any trails or even any lakes in the thick forest beneath us. All we could see were trees, distance, and far, blue mountains. A total silence held sway, as if we were the first people ever to be up there. Maybe we were. We sat down to rest and drink from our canteens.

Then we heard the most heavenly sound.

"A plane! Do you hear that? A plane! Where it is, oh, where is it?" I jumped up and shaded my eyes against the sun and turned around and around.

"There. See there, to the east. Airliner

bound for Salt Lake or Chicago, I guess."

"They don't see us!"

"They're way too high for that." But he kept gazing longingly after the little speck of plane, too. He looked down then, and put a brotherly hand on my shoulder. "A helicopter's what we want to see." He grinned in the sweetest way. "And I have a beautiful idea."

For a wild moment I thought the beautiful idea was to lean over and kiss me — I moved a little bit away, hating myself for being so flaky. "Which is?"

"We build a signal fire up here. I know there isn't any wood around, but we could carry it up. They'd see the smoke for sure."

"Yes! Yes! Brilliant!" I was so excited I danced up and down.

"How about I go down for wood and you wait here? In case they do come by. There's a good chance they'd see you, if you were running and waving."

"I'll run and wave till I drop. Okay, but hurry!" I couldn't tell him how panicked I was to be alone again. But of course one of us had to stay and keep watch. He could carry more wood than I could. Any minute, any minute now, I might see the helicopter looking for us!

Fifteen minutes by my watch went by. I counted the different kinds of flowers I could see as I walked around the little clear area. Three blues, a yellow, and a little star-shaped pink. By this time he should be back down. With the trail we'd made, it should take him about forty minutes to come back up with an armful of wood. The sky was terribly empty. Even the marmot had vanished.

I sat down on a rock to rest, and went over in my mind, spoonful by spoonful, the dinner my mother had made for me the night before we left. By the time I got to the desert, her gourmet chocolate sauce over ice cream, I could hear my stomach loud and clear.

Still an empty sky. Why weren't they out looking for us?

I stopped torturing myself thinking of food, and went over to check the markers we had made. There was the last duck, about five yards down the slope. It cheered me to see it.

By now over an hour had passed. I should never have let him out of my sight! What had happened? He was just dragging up a humongous load of big branches.

Or he had missed some of the markers, was off course, lost on the other side of the slope or — the bear had come back. I went down to the second marker and called as loudly as I could. "Phil! Phil! Phil!"

His name echoed back mockingly, just as my whistling had when I was first lost, which seemed a million years ago now. I knew I couldn't stand being lost alone again!

My hearing seemed to get abnormally strong. I could register every scrape of leaf, the twigs bending, almost hear flower petals shining in the sun. Once more I was all alone in the world.

Chapter 10

I had to go down there and find him. Maybe he had gotten sick, and that's why he was so slow. Or maybe searchers on foot were there! He was talking to them right now!

I followed the markers all the way down, hoping every second I would catch sight of Phil's plaid shirt or hear his steps on the rocks below. By now it was high noon and there were hardly any shadows under the boulders. The sky was still a bright, lively blue, without a cloud.

When I reached the grassy part at the bottom I could smell that heady mixture of flowers and wild onion. Even the birds weren't calling anymore. It was almost as if the world had stopped. All but me, still going, my heart tripping over itself.

I saw the black remains of our fire below the cave. No Phil.

"Phil!" I climbed up to the cave. Nothing but the pack, pad, and sleeping bag. I noticed I was crying out loud as I came down, long, cruel gasps that hurt my ribs. I couldn't bear it. He was lost — or dead!

"Phil! Phil! Phil!"

A groaning over by the pond, and there was a boot waving from a bush behind a big log!

"What happened, what happened? What are you doing there!" He was lying face-down in the brush.

"My foot's caught between some rocks," he moaned. I bent over him, pushing at the rocks until I had loosened his boot and lost my balance, pitching forward practically on top of him.

I wanted to put my arms around him and never let go, but instead, I got to my knees to try to help. He turned around slowly, keeping his left leg up in the air.

"Hey, you're crying." He looked stricken.

"I was afraid something had happened to you." I quickly brushed away the tears on my face and tried to smile. "I have this thing about being alone in the wilderness."

"I'm sorry you got scared," he said softly. I was still kneeling next to him, too relieved to move. I started to get up then, just as he did; our eyes met, and we stared at each other. His eyes were the liveliest green; up close like this I could see golden specks. He gave me a smile that could easily have wiped me out.

I wasn't about to let it. I got up briskly, which wasn't easy since my knees were like soup. "Phil, what happened?"

He seemed as relieved as I was to be talking. "I was just starting back" — he pointed to a huge pile of wood — "when I heard a noise over here. Fish jumping. This pond is wall-to-wall with big, juicy trout! I came out on the log for a better look, and it jostled loose, and I fell forward between those rocks, jamming up my ankle. Yeah, screw-up time again. I can't get up."

I pushed and heaved at the rocks until he could wiggle out. "Be careful, Phil. Don't put any weight on it. Here, put your arm on my shoulder; we can hop over to that log and take a look." As soon as he got his boot off, we felt his ankle carefully all over. Nothing seemed broken, but it was red and swollen. "Give me your headband." I dipped it in the water below us and wrapped it around the swelling. "I've heard somewhere that's a good thing to do. You'll have to stay off it."

"I know. I'll have to sit here and keep putting cold packs on it." He looked at me sadly. "You can't carry wood up there to keep a fire going."

"You just watch me carry wood! We've got to get a signal going!" As long as he was alive and all right, comparatively speaking, I felt I could do anything. "Well, since we don't have to waste time with lunch, I'll start back."

There was no help for it. If we were to have a signal, I would have to get it going.

He took out our little hoard of matches. "You're right, it's up to you now. Toss me that stick before you go?"

"I'll stay up there to keep watch, whether I get the fire going or not," I said bravely, not looking at him. "Me and the marmot. I know they're out looking for us." Was I really going back up there all alone? My mother would have died. Darcie and the girls wouldn't believe it for a minute. Bennet the baby taking charge!

A wave of glossy brown hair fell over his forehead. He didn't look at me, either.

"Well, see you when the sun gets low," I said jauntily. "Don't worry about a thing."

"Me, worry?" he said bitterly, and got out his knife to whittle on the stick. "We're going to have quite a story to tell them, aren't we?"

"We don't have to tell them *everything*."
He probably thought I meant something
besides the accident. "I mean, about your
ankle!" I gathered the wood and took off up
our path. To my surprise I found I was
glad to be by myself to do some thinking.

The first thing to get straight was that
nothing, *nothing* had happened. After all,
this was Phillip Hargrove! No, the looks
and silences between us were just sort of
reflex actions on his part. Something to
pass the time while lost in the woods. He
was going with Libby Lou, he kept reminding me of that, and the minute we were
found — oh, let it be this afternoon! — he
would be back with her. And a good thing,
too. A Sea Cliff type like him — he certainly wasn't for me.

But now that I was getting to know him,
he wasn't what I had always thought of as
Sea Cliffie. He wasn't stuck on himself, I
had to admit it. He was very brave — scar-
ing away that bear. Smart, too, figuring
things out. He had a great sense of humor;
you don't expect that in someone who's outright handsome. I thought again of the
beautiful shape of his nose, the way his
face lit up when he smiled with all those
perfect teeth.

But the main thing was he wasn't as

bossy as he had been; he was depending on me now just as much as I was depending on him. So what did it matter that he kept on doing kind of klutzy things? He wasn't my boyfriend and never would be. We were just partners for now.

It took me a long time, boosting that load of wood to the top of the ridge. The marmot was out, and watched me from a distant rock. Using some more pages from my book and a bunch of little twigs, I carefully, carefully built a fire. I held my breath and struck my match. It caught! I was in business with a signal.

As I settled down to tend it, I gave myself a serious lecture. I was in danger. Being lost, with practically no food, was a danger I could share with Phil.

Falling for him was something I couldn't share. I had to fight it on my own. He had Libby Lou; I wasn't any part of his real life, and we both knew that. He mustn't ever find out that I had this sick yearning for him.

From now on I'd be more businesslike. Friendly, but reserved. I had to keep reminding myself that he had a girlfriend; we were just partners out here.

It depressed me, coming to that conclusion, but I knew I was right. When my wood burned out, I walked up and down, scanning the sky.

As if in reward for all my straight thinking I saw it. A helicopter, coming out of the east!

Chapter 11

It shone like a silver eye, swooping to the south of me! I screamed and waved, waiting for it to circle. Found! Saved! Mom, Darcie — I almost passed out from pure pleasure, shouting and waving.

The helicopter kept going to a tiny glimmer, until I couldn't make it out anymore in the glare of the sun.

How could they not have seen me! I found my mouth was hanging open; I sat down heavily on the big rock. To be so near to civilization, home, safety, food. Less than a vertical mile away! Had it been too high to see me? Was the sun in the pilot's eyes?

I sat there a long time, trying to pump myself up again. *They'll be back, if not today, tomorrow. They're out searching and they're going to find us!* The marmot crept back out and watched me curiously.

I found myself wondering what he ate, and if it would do for us, too. I swallowed hard, trying to swallow my hunger and my disappointment.

If only the fire had still been burning, they would have seen me! I covered the ashes with dirt and stones.

When I started back down, the sun was almost to the top of the western peaks. I stopped often to take big swigs from my canteen, trying to fill up the emptiness inside. There would be nothing to eat until morning. I thought of the long, black night ahead.

It was all I could do to force a smile on my face when I got back. He was still on the log, wet bandanna around his ankle, fooling with the stick. "Phil, did you hear that helicopter? It came right over to the south of me, about two hours ago. It just kept on going. I couldn't believe it."

"Hey, no. But that's great news! The best news; they're out looking, and tomorrow they'll find us for sure."

I took another drink of water. "I'll be up there early, you better believe it. With more wood. I got the fire to go, but it burned out before they came. What are you doing with that stick?"

Phil had plunged it suddenly into the water.

He smiled sheepishly. "Trying to spear some of these trout. They're pretty fast, though."

I came over. After the rippling circles of water settled, I could spot a fish, then two fish — dark, marshy shadows twitching by right under us. I looked at them hungrily. Something clicked in my mind. "Be right back." I sprinted up to the cave, to my pack, remembering what I had seen pinned inside one of the pocket flaps. Yes! I rushed back down. "Look what I've got!" I waved it in front of him. "Ken must have forgotten it was there. What a miracle!"

If I had handed him the Hope diamond he couldn't have been more awestruck. "A fishhook. Bennet, you are fantastic. Now, what can we come up with for a line?"

I went back to the pack, and it didn't take me long to return with a spool of dental floss Mom had forced on me. Phil rigged up a line and fished, with me sitting hungrily beside him, until it was dark. Two faint little stars came out directly overhead and unseen frogs started to croak. Small birds began to flash through the shadows, whizzing right by our ears.

"What sweet little birds," I murmured. "It's almost as if they want to be near us."

"Bats." Phil said softly. "I mean, that's what they are. They won't hurt you."

Bats! I stifled a scream, covered my head with my arms, and started to move closer to him until I remembered that was a wrong move. I hoped the bats wouldn't come into the cave. Wasn't there something about caves and bats? I sat there rigidly, not daring to ask Phil. At last they skimmed away over the dark treetops.

"Good thing it's not really cold tonight," Phil said, after a while. "We don't need a fire, especially since we have nothing to cook."

"Right," I answered a little too heartily, trying not to think what would happen when we were out of matches, oatmeal gone, and still lost. My stomach was knotted in the usual dread.

"If you wanted to snuggle up close to me," Phil said kind of wistfully, "it would be warmer for both of us. We should conserve our body heat, you know."

"I'm not cold at all," I said quickly and falsely. I changed the subject at once. "Those fish don't seem to be going for Ken's hook, do they?"

"I've noticed," he said gloomily. "But people can live amazingly long times without food. The vital thing is water and we sure have enough of that."

"They're bound to spot us tomorrow, anyway. I'll take the pack full of wood besides what I can carry in my arms."

"Maybe I can limp up there with a load, too."

I doubted that, considering how he had to lean heavily on my shoulder to get back to the granite when it got too cold and dark to fish anymore. He crawled up to the cave on his own power and settled down with his poncho and pad. I got sadly into my sleeping bag.

"All set?" he called over. "Sweet dreams, partner."

But I couldn't go to sleep. I knew he was awake, too. "Are you thinking about food?" I finally asked.

"Stone-ground buckwheat waffles with blueberry topping, sausages, and at least five eggs, sunny-side up," he answered promptly. "I'm sitting there in a booth at Bunny's. I've just ordered it all over again, with another chocolate milk shake." He groaned. "We shouldn't do this, Bennet."

"Well, aside from food, what do you miss most? Your girlfriend, I suppose." It was pathetic to find myself on the subject of Libby Lou again.

He didn't answer right away. "She kept telling me not to go on this trip. She was so right."

"Not from my point of view." I thought

how I might have been dead by now, if he hadn't found me.

"She was upset anyway, because I wanted to drop out of Bonwell."

"Drop out of school!" I sat up in my sleeping bag, so amazed that I forgot how hungry I was. "Phil! Why would you do that?"

"Not out of school, just out of Bonwell. Money reasons. My dad had some bad business deals. He hasn't been able to pay my tuition. I don't like taking the money from my stepfather. I was going to check out public school, try to get into Lowell. My mother acted like I was plotting mass murder or something. Libby Lou got on my case, too."

"I know someone who's going to be a junior at Lowell. He's a real brain, too."

"Who is this brainy dude?"

"Darcie's brother. You know, my friend Darcie."

"The dude who loaned you the tent?"

"Right." There was something here I should think about, I realized dimly, back in my mind, something I didn't want to think about. Something to do with Darcie — I pushed it away.

"He's, ah, a special friend of yours?"

"Not really." Let him think what he wanted about poor old Ken. "So Libby Lou didn't want you to go to a public high school?" Being one of the great snobs of our time, naturally she'd have loathed that.

Of course he defended her. "She didn't want me to compromise my future, that was the reason. It's vital to have the best preparation for college you can get, she says."

"You would have gotten that at Lowell, believe me. If you were lucky enough to get in." I was being tactful. Lucky was not the word. You have to be really brilliant to get into that high school even if it is public.

"She has this dream of us going to the University of California at Santa Barbara. But it looks like there's no way my father can swing that, even if we had the grades, which we don't."

We, we. "What do you and Libby Lou want to study?" I asked sweetly, but my fists were clenched, my fingernails digging into my palms.

"She's going for public relations and advertising. My mother thinks I'm headed for law school back east, because that's what she wants. In a way, it's too bad I'm going with Libby Lou."

I propped myself right up on my elbows for this.

"Since I'm going with the girl Mother picked out for me, she's always been crazy about Libby Lou and her family, and she naturally assumes I'm going to do everything else she wants. Harvard Law School, that stuff."

"It's funny your mother's attitude didn't turn you off Libby Lou." As if the girl herself weren't enough to turn off anyone who wasn't sidetracked by tons of shining blonde hair, all those flashing teeth, mile-long legs. . . .

"For years it did. But she was like someone new when she came back from England."

With that phony accent. I actually put my hand over my mouth to keep from saying it aloud.

"It's kind of depressing to have your whole life programmed for you ahead of time," he went on. "I'd like a little space before I commit myself to law school. What about you?"

"Textiles," I said quickly. "I'm going to design fabrics."

"Oh, yeah, that book you brought along. Where do you want to go to college?"

"I'll have to go to San Francisco State. It's got a pretty good design department." I hesitated. "The best one is in New York, Cooper Union. But I'd be terrified to go there by myself."

"Don't make me laugh. You'd hit New

York like a swarm of killer bees."

"Really? Phil, do you really think so?" I smiled happily up into the dark. "My grandmother lives back there, too. But my mom would never let me go, not in a million years. I'd never have the nerve, anyway."

"You have nerves of steel, I happen to know. And the most beautiful blue eyes in California." His voice softened in a way that made my stomach dip.

"And you have the most beautiful girlfriend in California." That stopped him. "But I'm sorry you have money problems."

"Actually, I would kind of like to go to public school. From kindergarten on, I've always gone with the same crowd. Tahoe in the summer, Christmas parties, all that. At Bonwell it's the same. The Sea Cliff kids. Ordinarily, you and I wouldn't have gotten to know each other."

"Phil, why didn't Libby Lou want you to go on this trip?"

"Her family was going to their Carmel house this week. She wanted me to come along. Just think, I could be stretched out on that warm, soft sand, a double cheeseburger on one side of me — "

"And Libby Lou on the other."

He laughed. "She'd get a real kick out of you, if she knew you. You'd like her, too."

It was time again to be tactful. "Well, Libby Lou always seems to me kind of aloof. Maybe she's just shy." Shy! Darcie would have died laughing if she'd heard that. *Darcie*. Again I felt that little twinge. There was something I should think out.

"Not shy. I guess it's because she's always so involved in things, she doesn't have time to get to know other people."

Especially non-Sea Cliff people. "Don't worry about it, Phil. I can live without knowing Libby Lou. I didn't want to get to know you either, particularly." I turned the other way in my bag. "But I'm very, very glad I did."

"Thanks, partner." He said, in that gentle, well, *tender*, way again.

I pretended I was going to sleep and didn't answer. Tomorrow the helicopter would come back, and we would be home again. We wouldn't have any more conversations like this, probably never again. Instead we would be eating, eating — and I would be back in my own life. And then that little thought that had been trying to edge into my mind took center stage. *Darcie*. I was supposed to be taking notes on Phil for her!

I felt like the lowest of low traitors. I could hear her eager, thrilled voice now, asking about her beloved out in the woods.

And my evasive answers. How could I lie to her about the way I felt about Phil now? I'd never thought about lying to Darcie before. It just never had come up.

I had a hard time going to sleep. As soon as it was light, I would go up to the ridge and start the signal fire. It would be up to me to save us; Phil couldn't limp that far, let alone carry wood. I dozed off and woke with a start several times, then listened for his breathing before I could go back to sleep. When I woke up for good, I was alone in the cave.

The sun was coming up over the ridge. I scrambled into my jeans and boots and hurried down to where Phil was kneeling by the fire. "How's the ankle today?"

He picked up the stick he was using as a crutch, and hobbled a few steps. I could tell he was in pain. "The swelling's gone down a little. But I don't think I can make it up to the ridge. I'll stay here and try to get some fish. At least I can keep the fire going so we won't use up any more matches."

"And I'll take some fire up to the ridge in the pot." We grinned at each other as if I already had a huge signal fire blazing and the helicopter was landing. "Today is going to be the day!"

He had to hop on his good leg, leaning on

me, over to the tree where our two tiny bags of oatmeal were hanging, forlorn but safe. With me supporting him, he was able to use the stick to catch the knot and, finally, get the bags down. By that time I felt so faint I had to lean against the tree to steady myself. We really needed a meal.

While the water boiled we seriously considered eating the rest of the oatmeal. We decided not to do it. They *were* going to find us today, but until they did, we had to pace ourselves.

"If I could just get lucky fishing," Phil said hopefully.

"Keep trying," I urged. It was very good for his morale to have an activity like that while we waited for them to come.

After we ate I felt a shade less weak. Phil scrubbed out the pot and packed some coals in it for me. Together we hung the remaining oatmeal back up in the tree. I went off to wash. I could stuff both my hands in the front of my jeans, they were getting that loose. I checked my pale, smudged face in the little mirror I carried, and a wonderful idea hit me. I could signal with that mirror, too! People always did that in the mountains. I rushed back to tell Phil, who yelled and gave me a big hug.

I backed away quickly, trying to pretend it didn't affect me. "How about I blow

my whistle when I get to the top, and then
you blow yours? And I'll blow two long
times together when I sight the helicopter!
You do the same if you see searchers down
here."

"Right! This is it, partner. They can't
miss finding us today."

It took me a long time to get back up to
the ridge, carrying the pot of coals, sticks
of wood in the other arm, and the loaded
pack on my back. When I stopped to rest,
which was often, I admired the mauve haze
of a kind of flowering bush against the
bright, green grass. The wide, white petals
of another flower next to them reflected
the pink shadows cast by a big, red torch-
shaped flower next to it. I hadn't known
before this ghastly trip what wonderful
designs and colors nature came up with.
Like ice-gray granite in the shade of the
black-green pine tree, and the beige and
amber pine needles underfoot. It would be
great to be up here with a sketch pad and
watercolors, I found myself thinking. To
come back deliberately! I could hardly believe myself. And yet, someday, I might
just do that — staying at all times on a
well-marked trail, with at least a dozen
people always in sight.

The marmot wasn't around to greet me
at the top. I blew once on my whistle.

Faintly, faintly I could hear Phil's reply. Then I set to work building my fire. The coals took the paper and twigs right away; I was getting to be an expert. When it was going strong, sending up wispy trails of smoke, I sat down, mirror in hand, on what had come to be my rock, and began to wait.

It was only nine o'clock. There were oceans of time for the searchers to find us. I eyed a few tufty little clouds in the eastern sky, hoping the weather wasn't going to change before they got here. Only a dirty rim of snow was left under the trees, it had been so warm lately. I noticed a brand-new crop of fat, white flowers in a gray mat of leaves.

I couldn't help thinking of Mom. She was probably hospitalized from shock and worry by now. It would be on television and in the newspapers, I realized:

TWO BONWELL STUDENTS LOST IN SIERRA.

They wouldn't even know we were together until they found us today. There would be pictures of us — which one of mine had Mom given them? Not my middle school graduation one; I looked like a drunken owl. But I didn't really care, to tell the truth.

Why hadn't they found us by now? I stood up to tend my fire, and looked all around that vast sky again. Nothing. I sat down again. The smoke from my fire was very faint in the sunlight. Then I had another brilliant idea, and poured a little water from my canteen on the fire. Instant clouds of smoke! But they faded pretty fast. Should I do it again, and risk putting out the rest of the fire?

I wished I could confer with Phil about it. We worked well as partners now. I wasn't going to let myself fall in love with him. Up there in that bright, blinding sunshine I was sure I'd managed to escape that. I kept my eyes on the fire, feeding in the wood carefully. After all, there was Darcie. *She* was the one gone on Phillip Hargrove. Talk about disloyal. How could I explain being in love with him to her? I could see her now, yearning after him between classes with her big brown eyes, writing his initials all over her binders.

No, I'd just come back with a lot of exciting stories to tell her and the girls. I wouldn't tell everything. How we had been snuggled together, that first night in the tent, the way he had hugged me this morning. . . . I bet *he* wouldn't, either. Maybe our eyes would meet at school, and we'd both be thinking about the things we'd never told. . . . But we'd go our separate ways and eat our separate lunches. Big lunches. Peanut butter on nine-grain bread, with honey, and alfalfa sprouts. A huge, hard, red apple, the kind that spurts when you bite in.

I got up with a moan and walked around, scanning the sky. Out of the corner of my eye I saw my marmot had emerged from the rocks. I pretended not to notice him — her? — settling down to sun on the ledge. It was nice to have company.

By noon the fire was nearly gone and I had almost finished the water in my canteen. I had seen nothing, except a big, floppy-winged bird that could have been a vulture. By scrounging hard I managed to find a few dry twigs and coaxed a little more time out of the fire before it burned out. I thought again of the helicopter yesterday, that wonderful feeling that had rinsed through every inch of me when I saw it. I had felt it to the ends of my fingertips and toes. Found! Saved! And then it had gone on by — but at that moment I saw it again!

It was to the north this time, going back and forth — searching! They *were* looking for us! I put my whistle in my mouth but I decided not to give the signal until it got closer, until they swooped over and waved at me, to show they saw me, and were going to land. Then I would whistle the good news to Phil. I could just see that smile on his face!

I held out the mirror, waved it back and forth, shouting, running up and down, but they were too far away, going back and forth, circling, working their way over to me, to me! They would soon be coming nearer —

I watched the helicopter disappear over the eastern ridge of haze and mountain.

I found out then that there are times when you feel too bad to cry. I didn't think I would ever have the heart to move again. I had turned to stone.

I had been afraid before, but now a kind of endless, cold terror paralyzed me. They weren't going to find us today. There was a chance they would never find us. A very good chance.

We would get weaker and weaker, our two cups of oatmeal gone. Our matches gone.

This was all there was going to be, for Phil and me. I didn't have to worry about Darcie's feelings. We were going to die out here.

My water was gone, the sun was getting low, but still I sat, holding that stupid mirror. I couldn't shake this knowledge that we were reaching the end of the line. I couldn't deal with it, any way I turned. You aren't supposed to die before you're fifteen.

I heard Phil whistle below, and roused myself. One whistle, not two; no searchers had come down there, not that I expected them anymore. I put on the empty pack and made my way down the slope, noticing a cold little wind had come up. The clouds to the east were developing into something.

One way or another, these mountains were going to get us.

Before I could see our camp I smelled the woodsmoke. I wondered if Phil would be as down and scared as I was. He would know as well as I did that our hopes of being found were fading fast.

I tried to muster up a smile when he turned from where he was hunched over the fire.

"I thought you'd never get here. Look!"

Fish. Four big trout, cleaned and strung on sticks. Their sides gleamed, iridescent silver, pinks, blues.

"Here, take this one, keep turning it like a hot dog. We eat tonight!"

Like a baby, I cried. It was a bad habit I was getting into. My shoulders shook, the stick with the fish dipped practically into the fire, and tears ran down all over the place.

"Hey, please don't cry. Look, we're going to eat — let me hold that." But, instead, he put his fish down and held me in his arms. "It's *okay*, Bennet. I've got food for you now, you're going to eat! I made a bait out of roots; they really went for it."

"The helicopter came back," I sobbed, "but it didn't come near enough! They didn't see me!"

Phil stiffened. I knew he was thinking, too, they'd never find us. But he gave me a snappy smile. "We'll talk about that later. What you need now is fresh trout, okay? Hold the sticks, while I feed the fire." By the time he had revved up the fire, I had pulled myself together and sat down beside him to barbecue my fish. Every time our eyes met, we laughed like idiots, and sometimes I cried, too. It didn't matter. We were going to eat!

"I didn't think I could stand it until you got back," he told me as we watched our fish get crisp and brown. "I wanted to see your face when you saw real food. You're not going hungry anymore, partner."

Take it from me, there's nothing in this world as delicious as fresh trout barbecued over a camp fire. Except maybe a second fresh trout. When the fish were gone, we sucked the marrow from the bones. Phil said he would catch a big mess in the morning. "Hundreds of them in that pond, begging for my special bait."

"It was a meal I'll never forget," I said, licking my fingers. "I'd like to tell that father of yours what a fisherman you are. A whiz. A genius."

"You have my permission." He smiled proudly, and arranged a dogleg-shaped branch on the fire.

"I'll probably never have the chance." I tried to say it lightly. "Phil, they're not going to find us." Scary, scary words, but with my stomach full I could say them, thinking again of that deathly moment when the helicopter flew out of sight.

He frowned into the fire. "I don't think we can count on them finding us now, either. If we get back, we're going to have to do it on our own. And we *are* going to get back," he said fiercely.

"What about your ankle? And the high water?"

"Since I hardly walked on it today, my ankle's a lot better. It's good enough to go slowly. You can see how the water's gone down. I think we can make it. Especially now that we've eaten. What do you think?"

I got up and moved closer to him, scarcely realizing what I was doing. "We'll have to do it! It's scary, but we can't wait for them any longer."

"Right. Sure, we could stay here and live on the fish I'll catch, but they might never find us."

"It's up to us," I agreed. "We can do it; we have to." That little person inside me was back, covering her face and whimpering with terror. I had to ignore her.

"You better believe we can do it. Let's start tomorrow. I'll catch us a big breakfast and then we'll go. We can find our way, sighting from tree to tree, staying west. We're going to make it home." He smiled and then suddenly kissed me lightly. "That was just for luck," he mumbled.

"We might need a little luck." I moved quickly to the other side of the fire. We would need all the luck we could scrape up, to find the way back, to get across those streams.

I'd need an extra, secret portion of luck. I watched him as he banked the fire and buried the fish bones, using a stick of firewood for a shovel. His jeans hung on his hips, too, his hair was a wild, wavy mess, but he moved with confidence, crutch and all.

I could have watched him forever. He turned and his smile gleamed white in the dusk. "Ready to hit the sack, partner?"

I needed all kinds of luck, all right.

Chapter 12

"So tomorrow's definitely the day," I said as we took off our boots in the dark cave. I had to start powering myself up for it.

"Definitely," he agreed. "We're as good as crossing the Bay Bridge right now."

That brought up such a clear vision of the city, home, Mom — I couldn't answer over the lump in my throat. He was silent, too, probably thinking of Libby Lou's welcome.

"Funny, the way I never noticed you at school," he said in the dark.

"Not funny at all. We hung out with totally different crowds." It was all so far away now; Libby Lou seemed more or less a character in a movie I'd seen a long time ago.

"Still, I don't see how I could not have known you were there. I mean, you kind of stand out."

145

When there's nothing else around but trees . . . "You said I wasn't your type," I remembered.

"I was lying. We were fighting back then, you'll recall."

"You made a crack about my rotten personality."

"I was wrong. Bennet, I really admire your personality. It's dynamite. The best."

"I, I — your personality's okay, too." I turned dizzily the other way, almost overcome with pleasure.

He was silent after that. But the words he had said seemed to hang there in the cave, kind of echoing, for a long time. I slept deeply that night.

As soon as it was light Phil was outside. Thanks to having had real food, I felt strong for the first time in days. I was ready for another big fish fry, though. I tried not to think of the streams we'd have to cross, and would they be the right streams? If we did find our way back, how would we get across that big Mississippi-type river between us and the trail? There was no use panicking. We couldn't wait around any longer to be found; it wasn't happening that way. After he'd caught our breakfast we would go. I went off to wash and hurried back, ready to eat.

He was still over at the pond. "They're

not biting this morning," he said bleakly. "The little devils just swim on by."

The fire was blazing and ready. "There's always our delicious oatmeal."

"If we eat now, we'll only have one cup left."

We looked at each other, neither one wanting to say what we were both thinking. Two cups of oatmeal between us and starvation. But we were going to get back before that happened!

"Phil, I think we should eat half of it and get going. It's clouding over again."

"Right." He let me get it down from the tree where it hung. He was moving somewhat better than yesterday, but we wanted to save him any unnecessary steps.

The water finally boiled and we ate, which took all of thirty seconds. We checked directions against the tree marked "W" and started, just as the sun was coming up among the clouds.

We hadn't gone more than six yards when I saw Phil was in big trouble. Even with the crutch he could barely hop along. There was only one thing to do.

I went back to him. "Here. Lean on my shoulder. Come on, Phil. And give me that pack."

"I'm not going to have you help me back!"

"You've got to!" I was close to tears. "We won't make it at this rate. Please, Phil, don't be so macho! We're partners! You find the way, and I'll help you get there!"

He looked at me, and then laughed. "If you could see the fierce look on your face! Okay, partner. Your brawn; my brains." He let me take the pack and he put his arm around my shoulder and we started west slowly, but we were on our way. "Phil, the big woodsman, being towed home," he grunted.

I began to giggle. "By Bennet, the baby — if they could see me now!" It was hard work, supporting him and carrying the pack, but I was doing it.

I looked sharply around, trying to remember something, anything, to show we were going the way we had come.

But it all looked different. Flowers I had never seen before waved to the left and right of us. There was certainly a lot more water around; the pond stretched back into bushes I didn't recognize, either.

What if we were heading deeper into the wilderness, getting more and more lost? The oatmeal would be gone tomorrow. It was getting very cloudy. Catching fish last night was probably a fluke. He'd never be able to do it again.

I shook myself to get rid of these black, destructive thoughts, but they dragged at me in a kind of claustrophobic way. I felt I was suffocating under these endless, endless trees, from having been lost so long. I began to have trouble getting enough breath in my lungs, which scared me so much I had more trouble than ever. But I stumbled grimly along under Phil's arm.

"Hold it," he said. "Let's make sure we're going due west. Right. We must have crossed the stream about here."

"If you say so," I managed to say. Talking eased my tight chest a little, though. "I don't remember anything, I have to tell you."

"All right!" He gave a cry. "Look, see — that chunk of grass broken off the bank? I'm almost sure we did that."

"Phil!" I couldn't help it. Something desperate welled up in me. I flung my arms around him, and I guess he couldn't help it, either, because he closed his around me. I stared up into those bright, green eyes again. "Hey, I just — got a little spastic," I said weakly, drawing back before he could kiss me. I could see in his eyes that he wanted to. "Hoping so much we're on the right track here."

"We are." He touched my cheek with a filthy hand that smelled faintly of fish.

"You know what? I'm glad it was you I got lost with. I know that sounds crazy when I'm going with someone else — but this is a special circumstance. And you are one special girl."

I didn't know what to say. "Listen, we've got to get across this stream!" I felt strong again. In fact, my heart was singing, which was dumb, especially when I focused on all that deep, cold water we had to get across. "We'll have to wade?" He would rather be lost with me than Libby Lou! Wait till I told Darcie, and then, of course, I felt like a traitor again. I couldn't ever tell her any of this.

"We did it before. But it's worse, of course, after all the rain. We've got to test how deep it is." He inched in first, boots tied around his neck, probing the depth with the stick out front. I followed, minding the thick sludge and guck on the bottom almost as much as the freezing water, which came up over my knees, wetting my thighs and rolled-up jeans.

On the other side, we beamed at each other, although our teeth chattered as we unrolled our jeans and put boots back on. "We'll cross the next stream on the rocks, like we did before. I hope. Look around. Do you recognize this place?"

"I wish." I didn't see a familiar thing.

We could be getting more lost all the time. We could have crossed a totally new creek, and be going northwest instead of west. "Let's check direction again, Phil." There was no use waiting for a glimpse of the sun for that, since the clouds were getting thicker by the minute. We lined up the last tree with another one in front, and started pushing through marshy brush. I did remember marshy brush. There are probably hundreds and hundreds of miles of brush just like that in the Sierra.

"How about that?" He pointed triumphantly at the stones in the next branch of the stream. "We crossed here, I'm almost positive. I think I remember that big boulder there, with the roots hanging over it? We're going to be on that good old official trail home in a little while."

He had to be right. Of course he was right. Wonderful Phil, who was glad he was with me. Tears came to my eyes from lack of food and general suffering, I guess. All these lost, lost days — I blinked the tears back, and smiled encouragingly at him.

Then I took a good look at what we had to cross.

"When we get on the other side, we'll just follow the stream back to where we started down. We can't miss that spot." He was so sure he knew the way.

I could hardly bear to go on looking at this stream. The water boiled and hissed with such force fountains sprayed up between the rocks. Phil took the pack and limped out first, slowly. I held my breath, praying he wouldn't lose his footing. When he was almost over he took off the pack and threw it to the other bank, so he would be able to make the last, spraddling jump. "Your turn," he yelled when he was safely over.

I knew I had to do it. I tried to focus only on the rock below me, blanking out the foaming, roaring water.

The first rock was fairly level. Then with just an easy jump I made it to the next one, into a little pool of water on top, where pine needles floated.

I teetered a minute, keeping my eyes on the slick, white center of the last stone, knowing I must leap way out, not looking at the foaming water —

There was a sickening slippage under my boot, and I belly-flopped into the cold, roaring water. My mouth was full of sand as well as water, my lungs bursting, I felt a terrible pain — I was jolted to the surface again, slammed against a rock, Phil was shouting — silence. Blackness.

When I came to I couldn't breathe. I wasn't dead yet, but I was gasping, gasping for air, lying on the bank, aware that Phil was sitting on me, pounding my back. No air — a gush of water and sand poured out of my mouth onto the moss and mud. I could breathe again. I was conscious then of a throbbing pain in my shoulder.

"Bennet! Bennet!" He smoothed my sodden hair back from my face. "Are you okay? Don't try to talk."

"How did I get over here?" I spit out more sand.

He handed me his canteen so I could rinse my mouth. "The current, mostly. I managed to grab you when you came back up. Pure luck. You've got to get out of those wet clothes right away." He pawed through the pack for dry tights and socks, my rain gear. "Here! Strip all that off and put these on."

He helped me get my wet boots off and then turned away so I could do the rest myself. I still felt clammy, but it was better than the sopping, freezing clothes. The rhythmic pulsing of the pain in my shoulder was the only warm part of me. "Okay, I'm ready to mush on." The sky was a dark, seething gray now. I felt cold clear to my bones. "Lean on my other shoulder, for a change, Phil." If he knew I was hurt, I knew he would refuse to lean on me at all.

We limped along, crawled up the brushy side of a huge boulder, slid down what appeared to be a sheer drop on the other side. None of which I'd ever seen before. "You remember this!" Phil insisted. "Pretty soon we'll see the spot where I was when I first called to you, on the other side of the stream. And from that spot, we can see the trail!"

I prayed that we could. But I had a swelling, relentless, coming-to-the-end-of-the-rope feeling. My head seemed to belong to someone else. Everything around us looked strange to me, except the sky. It was black and boiling in a way I remembered all too well.

The first raindrops hit us. I staggered and almost brought us both down.

"You all right? Once we're on that trail, Bennet, we can make it back to Hunters' Lake in two or three hours. There may be searchers and backpackers there."

I tried to tell him he was wrong. But something thickening seemed to have happened to my tongue and mouth. I was beginning to feel deliciously warm, so warm I longed to sink down on the sloshy ground — the rain was getting very heavy now — and fall asleep. Just a little nap, right here. "Resshtime," I tried to say.

He turned and looked at me. Let him get mad, I thought, marvelously no longer connected with this scene. It didn't concern me anymore. I could tune it all out, fall into a deep healing sleep . . .

Phil was slapping me!

"Bennet! Come on! You've got to keep walking! You're getting hypothermia! Come on! Walk! Walk!" He prodded me with one arm, hopping on the crutch with the other. If I'd had the strength I would have laughed, even as I fell back into my sleep. He pushed me under a tree. "Stay there, out of the rain, while I get the tent up — and take this!" He stripped off his poncho, and slipped his down jacket around me. "I'll be as fast as I can! Take a drink of water. Drink! You've got to stay awake. Please stay awake! You can't go to sleep with hypothermia!" There was a high, raw note in his voice. I tried to stand, but the ground, pine needles, leaves, and mud, came softly up to meet me.

"Oh, no! Bennet! Talk. Talk to me! Stay awake!"

The next thing I remember is being hauled into the tent, my boots removed, and being thrust into the sleeping bag. There was something I had to tell him! *We put up quite a fight, Phil. But we lost. Talk about your overwhelming odds* — more lost than ever; the rain outside roaring down again. Starving, his beaten-up ankle, my shoulder. . . .

From far off I could hear his voice. "Bennet, Bennet! Answer me! Tell me your name and address!" From my cozy depths I registered that was weird. Did he want to send me a letter? I was far too sleepy to answer. But he kept slapping my cheeks as I slipped further away into my nice, warm darkness. "I have to do this — I have to keep you awake! Answer me!"

I might have murmured, "I love you, Phil." I remember thinking it, and smiling in my sleep. The rain had stopped lashing and a Hawaiian-type sun was baking me. I was getting warmer and warmer in my bikini. "I'll burn if I don't get out of this sun," drifted through my mind.

The sun was shining through the tent wall. I was in my sleeping bag, and Phil was in the tent with me, his worried face peering into mine.

What thick eyelashes he had, like sable brushes. "You're okay! Bennet, you're okay! When someone starts to get hypothermia you've got to get them warm."

"You really have a thing about saving my life today," I said weakly. It wasn't much of a joke, but I had to say something to keep from bawling like a baby.

The most beautiful tenderness came into his voice. "I wasn't going home without you. No way. Bennet, I was so scared! I was so afraid you'd die — but you're okay, now! I'm going to make a fire. You need hot food."

I certainly needed something. I felt as weak as a kitten. "Who around here doesn't? But we shouldn't use up any more oatmeal today."

"It doesn't matter, we're all but on the trail! I'm going to hunt for some dry wood."

I knew that he was wrong. We weren't ever going to find the trail again. But it took too much effort to think about all that. We were going to die here. At least we would be together. I must have fallen asleep again because the next thing I knew Phil was pushing a pot through the tent flap.

"Hot soup is served. You've got to drink it all."

I sat up, and Phil fed me spoonful after magnificent spoonful. "What did you do? It's marvelous. I love it. Oatmeal soup!"

"Sometimes I'm touched with genius, I admit it. It came to me that we could stretch our supply — and you had to take in a lot of liquid. A natural."

"You eat some, too."

"I'm not hungry," he lied. "Go on, drink it up. You'll need your strength for the homecoming."

"Don't I wish." I pushed the pot firmly toward him. "That's all I want, honest. Please drink the rest. Or let's save it, in case we're not back, after all." I didn't want to tell him, just yet, that I knew we were more lost than ever.

"We're back. *We are back.* Look, Does this convince you? I found them hanging in a tree over there, where we put the tent up the first night."

His binoculars. It was as if civilization had reached out and tapped me on the shoulder. I touched them wonderingly. That lovely, city-looking, damp leather case; I had to open the case and take them out, almost crying at the solid black and chrome weight in my hand. "We *are* going to get home! All we have to do is wait for the water to go down — "

"We don't have to wait! A giant tree has fallen across the main stream; I saw it when I was out hunting for wood. We can whiz right across! We're home free!"

"Let's go! What time is it?" I made the mistake of putting weight on my shoulder and cried out.

"Hey, let me take a look at that." Delicately he prodded my shoulder. Rain began beating down again. We looked at each other and laughed.

"Another reason why we'd better wait a while. You'll feel a lot stronger after a little rest. Then we'll charge across that stream. We'll do it. Believe me."

I did. I believed him. We were going to make it! "You saved my life. Again."

"My pleasure. Oh, Bennet, if it weren't for Libby Lou — " he sighed.

We lay listening to the rain.

"I'm always going to love the sound of rain, because it'll make me think of you," I said sadly and simplemindedly. "Don't feel bad, Phil. There's a reason why I can't get involved with you, too." Darcie. I couldn't take over her beloved.

He turned to look at me. "What reason?

"I'd rather not say." There was no way I was going to tell him about Darcie's passion for him. I might be a dope and a klutz, but I had some decency. I wasn't a groupie like Darcie, though. She had it bad for some fantasy person she'd more or less made up. But I was in love, I might as well admit it privately to myself, with a real-live Phil, all six feet and probably no more than 140 pounds of him now, right next to me, smelling of woodsmoke and sweat. I was in for a lot of pain, I could see that, too. And I wasn't thinking about my shoulder.

"That Ken dude, right?"

"Ken?" I asked stupidly. "Ken. Oh, no, hey, no. He's just Darcie's brother."

"I wish things were different, Bennet."

I thought of running into him and Libby Lou, hand in hand, between classes. At least that wouldn't be until September. But Darcie would be after me the second I got back, wanting all the details about her adored one, her Phillip Hargrove. Would she catch on that I wasn't telling the whole story? How could I not tell everything to Darcie? Stonewall *Darcie*?

"I've learned a lot of things out here. One: partners are closer than girlfriends," he said. "I've never had a partner before."

"Me, either. Out here it's just you and me. But it's very complicated, back there in the world."

"Don't I know it. But for now — "

"For now, we're partners and we belong together." I know, I know. It was dumb. But I just couldn't help myself.

We listened to the rain beat on the tent wall slanted above us. Cold, wet, hurting — and happy because we were still together.

Chapter 13

When the sun came back out we drank the last of the oatmeal soup and got underway again. I felt marginally stronger, but I could hardly use my right arm. Every time I moved it I was almost shot down by the pain. Phil made me a sling out of his bandanna. He wouldn't admit it, but I knew his ankle was worse.

My jeans and jacket were as wet as they were when he dragged me from the stream. He insisted I wear his down jacket under my rain clothes. "I've got all these other great, warm, dry things on, like my jeans and shirt, Bennet."

"Your socks are wet, though," I pointed out, "from when you jumped in the water. *I've* got the dry socks that were in the pack. Nyah, nyah." We stopped putting on boots and shook with giggles.

"Anyway, Phil, I feel warm all over."

He felt my forehead. "No wonder. You're running a fever." He made me rest some more while he took down the tent.

"Okay, partner." He dropped the tent roll in the pack. "On to the trail." We walked, Phil limping on his own now, to the stream, and there was the big tree he'd described, fallen almost across.

My heart sank. He hadn't mentioned that it was about twelve feet above the raging stream, and didn't look at all steady.

"You can see where it's been split off, by lightning, I bet," he said. "Look, there are chunks of it all over the place. It must have made quite a bang when it came down."

We looked at the huge pieces of branches littering both sides of the stream and sniffed the nice, clean smell of cut wood.

"We can zip right across on that, Bennet. No problem."

There was no way out of it. We would have to cross on that tippy-looking tree trunk, way up there above the boiling, frothing water, and a good yard short of the other side. This stream was twice as wide and at least twice as ferocious as the one I'd just wiped out in.

I knew I couldn't do it, not with my painful shoulder. One false step — no, I couldn't do it! I simply wouldn't be able to force my body to climb up and out on that horrible tree, which looked more dangerous every second. I opened my mouth to yell above the water, to tell him he would have to go back without me, leave me here alone — and then I realized he'd never make it back without me to lean on.

Phil had started over, crutch and all. He inched along. The tree lurched, and I almost threw up. "Nothing to this," he bellowed. "Now when I get here," — he had reached the gap at the other end between the trunk and bank — "I simply jump" — he soared over the open, ranting, snarling water, and landed on his bad ankle. I cried out at the pain he was feeling, but in a minute he got up and motioned me to come.

"I can't jump that far!" I called, almost breaking down, knowing I would have to do it. To complete the misery, the rain was falling again, rustling in the bushes, wetting my hands.

"You won't have to! I'll hold out the stick when you get to the end of the log for you to grab!"

Even now I get nightmares, thinking about that tree. My legs were shaking so much I could hardly climb up to take the first step. Or the second step. Then I made the mistake of looking down, at the big, red-brown pieces of tree bark under my boots and seeing that black, seething water way down below.

I froze. I couldn't go forward and there was no way I could turn around to go backward.

I could only shake, beginning to sway over — I couldn't do it! Not that way. I sat down, straddling the log, and inched myself along, using my good arm, eyes closed, pushing on blindly, too terrified to make much progress. Minute after minute of torture, knowing I would soon fall, my stomach in my throat —

"Come on, Bennet, you can do it! You've done everything else; you can do this, too. Come on!"

I forced myself to open my eyes. I was near the end of the trunk, to where I would have to jump. I shuddered and clutched the log tighter with my knees.

"Here! Reach out for the stick!" Phil waved it in front of me.

To get it I would have to stand up. For a long moment I couldn't make myself unfreeze my death grip on that log. At last, knowing I had to do it, the water waiting below, I balanced shakily on my knees, then got to my feet —

"You've almost done it! Now reach!"

I lunged through the gray slush of rain, flailing horribly in the air, grabbed the stick, and stood beside him on the bank! My shoulder humming with pain, but the rest of me in paradise. Together we would make it!

He hugged me to him. "Yahoo! I knew you could do it! Okay, let's make tracks — the trail's right over here; I swear to you it's right over here someplace." The rain was falling very heavily now.

"Bennet." Through the rain he pointed to one of the most gorgeous sights in the Western world.

A pile of three stones. A duck. And three yards below it, another pile of stones, and another. We were on the trail! WE WERE ON THE TRAIL!

No, I was dreaming. I would wake up in the cave again. But my shoulder was hurting too much for this not to be real life.

We were on our way home.

"First stop, Emerald Pool." Phil limped along slower than ever. "Where we had lunch. You remember Emerald Pool."

We lurched on. The beauties of good old Emerald Pool were lost in the rain, but soon after that the sky began to clear. Now we could see down the valley, to the woods we'd hiked through, that long-ago far-off morning — *four* days ago? It could have been a million years back.

"Oh, look, Phil!" It was a gum wrapper

on the trail. I bent down reverently, and picked it up. Humans had passed this way. "It might be from our trip."

"I hope no one at Bonwell is gross enough to litter the wilderness. Hey, you know what I'm going to do with my life? I've just decided."

Your life will be with Libby Lou, I thought wearily. It's all planned out, you said so.

"I'm going to go into the forest service. Be a ranger. And you know what else? I'm going to specialize in finding lost people. They need some serious reorganizing in that department. Hey, look at me. Smile."

"What for, you dork?"

"I just wanted to see those cute little teeth. No one else has a smile like yours." We stopped in the rain. "How I'm going to miss you."

"Phil, we've got to keep moving."

"Right. It won't be long now." He staggered heavily forward, almost falling in the mud. I knew his ankle must be killing him.

"You've got to lean on me again, Phil! Here, on my good shoulder."

"I'm just too heavy for you."

"You're just right for me." I didn't even try to take that back; I meant it in every sense of the word. "Please! We'll make better time together."

We limped on, his arm on my shoulder, my arm around his waist. Flashes of sunlight occasionally lit up the granite around us, and the tops of the dark green trees we could see at the end of the valley.

"They must have all given up and gone back to the city," he muttered.

But I knew that couldn't be true. Mom would have had search parties out looking for me for ten years from now. "What if there's no one at Hunters' Lake?"

"We'll go on back to the trailhead. We'll hitchhike back to the city. We'll get there if we have to walk every step of the way."

"Lurch every step of the way." I giggled but it turned to tears. Rock and bushes, trees and clouds, washed in and out of focus. The only solid, permanent thing in the world was Phil's weight on my good shoulder.

"Within striking distance now, partner," he kept saying.

I stopped so suddenly he crashed against me. "I'm hallucinating. No! Look up there! Phil! Those are people!"

Five people on foot and five more on horses were coming down a trail on the other side of the valley. "People." I hadn't known before how distinctive, how powerful and important, human beings looked out in the woods.

Phil dug out his whistle and blew, loud sets of three. They blew back.

They had seen us!

We stumbled on as quickly as we could, watching the people on horseback gallop up the trail: A ranger was in the lead. With a whoop he slid off his horse and rushed up to us.

"Both of you! WHOO HEE! Welcome back! We sure been combing the watershed for you two! There's going to be some mighty happy people in Three Streams — " he reached for his radio. "Your families," he explained, "there at search headquarters."

At that point things got jumbled. I do remember they put us on horses and one of the people on foot was Mr. Quillan. The poor man stood there babbling. "You were together! Swept away by the flood; I knew it couldn't be true. Both of you! I prayed it couldn't be true! You're all right, both of you are all right!" There were tears in his eyes.

At the trailhead they transferred us to a waiting ambulance. We sat on the cot, Phil's arm locked around me. With siren roaring, the ambulance raced down to the hospital in Three Streams.

"Okay, young lady." A paramedic or someone whipped open the back door before we came to a full stop, and lifted me into a wheelchair.

"I can walk! Where are you taking me? Where's Phil going?"

"You'll see him later, after we look you over." He pushed me rapidly into the hospital, where lots of people were waiting. I turned from the crowd to see Phil being wheeled away down another hall.

As they whisked him out of sight, he shouted, "I'll be in touch, partner!"

Mom. Inside my hospital room we hugged and cried, both talking at once.

Mom couldn't let go of me. She had new wrinkles in her cheeks, and I think she was running a fever, too. Her eyes were wet and flashing. "I thought I'd lost you, I thought I'd lost you. My baby, oh, my baby!"

I don't remember all the details of getting cleaned up and x-rayed. Finally, they put me in a nice, clean bed. I'd totally forgotten how soft and heavenly beds are. An IV was strapped to my arm, and the nurse placed a tray in front of me, with a beautiful bowl of steaming soup. Would you believe oatmeal soup? I let go of my mother's hand and had a sputtering fit. "Oh, Mom, where's Phil? I bet they gave it to him, too!"

The nurse looked disappointed. "Dear, we have to start you on light foods." She tried to make me take a pill, to calm me down.

I pushed the pill away. "Oatmeal is all we had to eat for days! Oh, it's so strange to be eating without him." I took a few sips of the soup, which was a hundred times better than ours.

"Go to sleep, honey," Mom crooned when the soup was taken away. "I'll sit right here by you, until you drop off. . . ."

"So strange to sleep without Phil," I murmured, drifting off, registering too late that my mother was giving me an odd look.

In the morning they took out the IV and let me have a real, heavenly breakfast of scrambled eggs, toast, juice, cereal, and bananas. The nurse brought in the newspapers so I could read all about us getting lost. They *had* used my dippy middle school graduation picture, on TV, too, they told me. Diagrams and maps showed all the places they had looked after the storm was over. There had been a growing fear that we had drowned in the swollen streams. "I would have been, but Phil pulled me out."

Mom groaned and grasped my hand tighter. "I should never, never have let you go on that trip!"

"It was scary and awful, sure. But Mom," I really wanted her to hear this, "I found out how strong I really am."

"We could sue the school for negligence! Taking helpless teenagers into the wilderness."

"It was my own fault I got lost! And we weren't helpless! Mom, we found ourselves, did you notice that? We got back to that trail on our own." I felt so well I got up and dressed in the new jeans and plaid shirt Mom had bought while I slept the day before.

"And those reporters," Mom went on. "You're in no condition — I finally agreed that they could talk to you and the Hargrove boy for a few minutes when we check out. But only if you want to, honey! I'm not going to let you get exhausted."

"Mom, I don't mind." I would get to see Phil soon, then.

Dee and Mollie phoned. They told me that Mr. Quillan marched them all back to the trailhead practically before daylight the morning after we got lost, and called the rangers out. The kids had waited around all day before they were bussed back to the city.

"We died a thousand deaths," Mollie reported. "We couldn't do anything but watch the news, cry, and phone each other. Everyone was like that. What an ordeal."

"That's the word," I agreed. No one would ever know that I was partly lying. "How's Darcie?"

"Much better. It was mononucleosis. She had to go to the hospital for a lot of tests. Ken says she can have visitors tomorrow."

She'd be phoning any minute. I felt terrible twinges of guilt.

But when the phone rang, it was Phil.

"How's it going, partner?"

It was so good to hear his voice. "Terrific. My mom's here — listen, my collarbone was broken, but they didn't have to set it. I'm in a kind of vest. What about your ankle?"

"Torn ligament. And guess what, I'm in a giant cast up to my knee. Is that wild?"

"Wild," I agreed. "Are your parents there?"

"My mother, my stepfather, and my dad. They're in the cafeteria now." There was a pause. "Libby Lou is with them."

"So, how is she?" It was amazing how quickly the brightness went out of the day.

"She's fine. Bennet, I had a long talk

with all three of my parents. I told them forget law school. I'm going to study forestry and all that. They took it pretty well, though I don't think Mother believes it's for real. Hey, my dad and I are planning a giant backpacking trip in August. Want to sign on?"

I laughed. To tell the truth, if it had been a serious invitation I would have jumped at it. I would come back to these mountains like a shot, to be with Phil.

"I wish life were less involved," he said sadly.

"It will be. We're back now."

"I missed you so much last night."

Neither of us spoke for a while.

"Well," I said at last. "I hear we're checking out at two."

"Oh, yeah," he said eagerly. "I'll see you then. How about that press conference, partner? We'll knock 'em dead."

"Will we recognize each other in dry clothes?" I hung up, so happy, in spite of Libby Lou, I could hardly keep from hugging the nurse when she came in to weigh and measure me some more.

I refused the wheelchair Mom had ordered, and walked out to the hospital steps on my own, Mom hovering anxiously.

For a second I didn't recognize Phil in a huge white cast. And with Libby Lou —

looking more beautiful than ever in a big peach sweater, blonde hair swooping over her pearly cheeks — hanging on him. His mother and stepfather were on the other side, and behind Libby Lou was a tall man with an elegant nose just like Phil's. As soon as he saw us he came over.

"I'm Phillip Hargrove's father," he said putting a hand out to Mom. "So this is the brave young lady Phil's been telling us about." He took my hand, too. "Bennet, I thank you for bringing Phillip back to us alive."

"Oh, hey — no! He was the one who saved me. Mr. Hargrove, Phil was wonderful in the woods! He saved me from drowning, and hypothermia — "

"The boy did well, I must say. But he told us he wouldn't have made it without your courage and resourcefulness." He turned to Mom. "I must congratulate you on having such a mature and cool-headed daughter."

Mom looked stunned.

"Mr. Hargrove!" I remembered something important as he turned to go. "I wanted to tell you what a magnificent fisherman Phil is! The only decent food we had all that time was the fish he caught! He's a totally marvelous fisherman!"

A strange look came over Mr. Hargrove's face. And then he smiled. Maybe he guesed that Phil had told me about their disastrous trip together. "Thanks, Bennet. Phillip did mention the fish."

Then the reporters gathered around. We told them about the bear getting our food, the signal fires up on the ridge — "Bennet's signal fires," Phil pointed out. "She carried the wood up there and did them by herself." "You caught the fish!" I said. "And rescued me from drowning. And then saved me from hypothermia." Frankly, I loved seeing them write all that down.

"But I wouldn't have been able to walk out of there on my own. Bennet towed me out," Phil told them. "She's a real tiger." Our eyes met and we laughed. So did everyone else, except Libby Lou. The video cameras were trained on us, and flashbulbs flashed. I noticed Mom had the strangest look on her face.

After it was over, Libby Lou turned to me.

"I just simply will nev*ah* be able to thank you enough, Bennet *dah*ling, for returning him home to me," she gushed. "It seems you're this outright whiz! In the woods. Just like being with Quack Quillan, Phillip says."

It wasn't like being with Quack Quillan! Phil couldn't have said that! I looked at him, still caught in a group of reporters, and suddenly felt sick and weepy.

"I'll tell him good-bye for you." She nodded graciously and went over to lock herself on to Phil's arm.

Whatever he had said, he was Libby Lou's. Our partnership was over; I had to remember that.

I had to get used to the idea that we were back in our separate lives again.

Chapter 14

"Honey, what you've been through."
Mom steered the car carefully down the
mountain road. "I still haven't taken it in.
But one thing's clear." She smiled over at
me, a little sadly. "I have lost my little
girl."

"Mom!"

"Oh, yes. When I saw how you handled
yourself with those reporters — I didn't
dream you could speak in front of a crowd
like that. To say nothing of the things you
did out there! That boy actually said he
wouldn't have survived if it hadn't been for
you. You're no longer my baby. I've got to
remember that." She gave me another,
well, admiring look. "Your father would
have been so proud — I think you can do
just about anything!"

It reminded me of what Phil had said —
"You'd hit New York like a swarm of killer

bees." I didn't say anything to Mom, but I knew then that I *was* going to go to Cooper Union when the time came. It was an exciting idea; I stopped thinking about Phil for a while. I'd tell Darcie, of course — Darcie. I'd need some strength and smarts to deal with that situation. Phil was far removed from both of us, but he was still Darcie's beloved. I noticed then that I was suddenly very tired.

When we got home I went through all the rooms, getting used to being back in my life. I must say, our cat Gullie was pretty cool about seeing me. But I had to kiss her and touch everything, my drawing board, my phone; I opened my closet to check on my clothes.

The phone rang nonstop. Every girl I'd ever known called me. After going through how horrible it had been, they all got around to the key question. What was it like being lost in the woods with PHILLIP HARGROVE?

"You know," I'd say, hurting, sure, but I could soon say it both earnestly and casually, "he's a nice guy? Lucky for me, he knows a lot about the wilderness. He saved my life more than once."

"Oh, really?" They were all disappointed, wanting to hear juicy stories of us fighting, or falling in love. . . .

Mom made my favorite Hawaiian chicken for dinner. We had to shut the phone off so we could eat, there were so many calls. None of them were from Darcie. But I knew she had been trying to get through. It was dumb, feeling guilty as if she somehow knew I'd fallen for her beloved and was already mad at me.

After dinner we watched the news. There we were on the Three Streams Hospital steps. I could hardly take my eyes off Phil. I noticed that Libby Lou had managed to get in the picture, smiling adoringly up at Phil. After all, she *was* his girlfriend.

He called the next morning before I was out of bed.

"Just checking how you got through the night. Thinking about us in the cave." There was a pause. "Do you remember?"

"I'm planning to forget, though." I rolled over, and had to work to keep the smiles out of my voice.

"Bennet, listen. I tried to talk to Libby Lou last night. But I can't seem to get through to her. It got very heavy. She cried and told me she loves me, all that stuff." He sounded very gloomy.

"So what's the problem? It's over, and all is forgiven." My throat was suddenly as tight as a fist.

"It isn't over. You know it isn't."

"Phil, we'd better face it. It is. I have to go now." I hung up quickly, seconds before Mom appeared at the door.

She had planned for me to spend the day in bed. "You don't recover from an ordeal like that overnight, honey!"

I just smiled and went on dressing. "I have to see Darcie," I reminded her. "And take back Ken's gear. It's only in the next block."

"No need, honey. You stay in bed today; I'll bring the things back for you."

"Mom, I feel fine. I want to see Darcie."

Mom kept on protesting as she served me waffles, sausages, and fruit compote. "Honey, there's no reason."

"There's reason." I put down my fork. "Remember what you said in the car? I'm not a baby, Mom. You were going to remember that."

She went out to get more sausages, a hurt look on her face. I almost ran after her to say I didn't mean it. Luckily the phone rang.

"That must be Darcie." I leaped up to get it.

It was Phil again.

"What did you have for breakfast?"

After I told him, he told me all the things he'd eaten, and what he planned to eat. "We're taking my dad to his plane now."

"Libby Lou's coming with you?" It was dumb to ask.

"Uh, yeah. She wanted to come." Neither of us said anything for a long time. I curled and uncurled the slippery phone cord around my fingers.

"She doesn't understand I'm not the same person I was before."

"I know what you mean," I said softly.

"Sometimes I almost wish we were back up in the woods," he said. "Things were simple. You, me, a bear or two."

I saw I would have to do it. "Phil, do me a favor? Don't hit the phone anymore, okay? It'll be easier for both of us."

There was another silence. Then he said, "I know I don't have any right to call you, the way things are."

"You've got it. It's been great knowing you, Phil. Good-bye." I said as brightly as I could, and hung up. Closed chapter. End of book. I went out to the kitchen and gave Mom a big hug to muffle the sadness pouring through me. "I missed you so much. Mom, will you do something for me?"

"Anything, darling. Anything!"

"Teach me to cook this summer? Let's start with your dynamite waffles." She agreed, feeling better, I think. It was one thing to say I wasn't her baby anymore; it was another to remember it. I would have to expect backsliding; go a little slow, give her a chance to adjust. Feeling mature, I decided it would be my number one summer project. To ease her into it, I asked her to phone Darcie while I got dressed, and I let her drive me over.

I went up Darcie's steps with a stomach full of moths. Talk about feeling crummy. She would be dying for every last juicy detail of my days, and nights, with her beloved. Of course, I couldn't let her know I'd fallen in love with him. But she'd spot right away that I was keeping something back. It took me the longest time to ring the bell.

Ken opened the door and took the pack from me, blushing madly. "Great news. That you got back," he finally managed, not meeting my eyes. "Darcie's resting in her room." I felt him watching me as I sprinted upstairs, just like I always did, as if I couldn't wait to see her.

She leaped to the door, and we half-hugged, favoring my bad shoulder. "They didn't even tell me you were lost! Daniel thought it might be too traumatic — my best friend lost, alone in the mountains!"

"Well, I wasn't exactly alone." I thought

I better admit that much, up front. "Who's Daniel?"

Darcie's cheeks turned red and her voice deepened. "Daniel. My doctor. Bennet, he actually came out here to the house. And the minute he walked in — he's about thirty, but he looks young, that kind of thin, intense look? I don't think he eats enough, he's so devoted to his patients. I have an appointment to see him this afternoon. Only four more hours. He came out here to see me the first time! And I saw him at the hospital when I had all those tests. Most doctors aren't that devoted when you have mono, am I right?"

I sat down, with barely enough strength to pick up one of her teddy bears. I straightened its red satin bow. "You call him Daniel?"

"He said I could. I'm going to medical school. I know, I know, I have that problem with biology, but I can lick it. I'm going to devote my life to humanity, like Daniel has. I plan to tell him today. That way, see, I can ask him a lot of personal questions about where he went to school, and what courses I should be taking. After all, I can't expect to have mono forever. I've got to line up some reasons to keep phoning him."

"Darcie! Don't you want to hear about me being lost? With," I made myself say it,

"Phillip Hargrove? Your beloved?"

"Oh, him. Did he give you a bad time? When they finally told me, I just about died, Bennet, and Daniel prescribed something to calm me down. When I woke up they told me you were found. I just about died." She hugged my good side again.

"We found ourselves, you know. Darcie. This is Phillip Hargrove I'm talking about!"

"That child." She sighed "I must have been out of my mind. A stuck-up snob, you were so right about that."

"He's not stuck-up!" I snapped. "He saved my life more than once. He's a totally marvelous person."

She raised an eyebrow. "If you say so. Did I tell you Daniel has these dark, burning eyes? I wish you could see his hands." She smiled blissfully.

"I'm trying to tell you something! I really — got close — to Phil. We had a terrific time together, when we weren't scared out of our gourds. He liked me. A lot."

I had her attention at last. "Fantastic! But what about the Queen of England? What about Libby Lou?"

I fiddled with the teddy bear's bow. "He'd like to break up with her, I think. But. Well. She's been his girlfriend for so long. She understood and forgave him."

"That swine. Oh, Bennet, I've been there. Don't I know the pain you're feeling? But remember, he's only a high school kid, for Pete's sake. He isn't worth it."

"Actually, he is. He really is. But I told him not to phone me anymore, as long as he's going steady with her."

Darcie nodded and settled back on her pillow. "You're back in the real world, never mind what happened up in the mountains. He'll never dump Libby Lou; those two Sea Cliffies belong together. And you'll get over it." She hugged me carefully, and it was a full minute before she started talking about Daniel again: "Hands of a surgeon, really, but he's in general practice because he believes in the whole patient." She smiled out into space in that goofy way I knew so well.

I thought about what she said when I walked home a couple of hours later. *You're back in the real world. He'll never dump Libby Lou.* I knew him well enough to know he would keep his word; I couldn't expect him to phone anymore. If he couldn't bring himself to break off with her, wasn't it because deep down he didn't want to? Or maybe he did now, but in a few days he wouldn't anymore?

I realized then that you can love someone even though you're really disappointed in him and afraid he doesn't love you back like he should.

Like he did when we were lost together.

But I wasn't about to mope around, groupie style, like Darcie! I'd get over him, somehow. Learn to cook, get Mom used to the idea I wasn't the same babyish nerd I'd been before I got lost. My heart wouldn't keep on being this much of a problem forever.

The sky was that stinging, clean, blue it gets here when the fog burns off early.

There are days when you just know deep in your bones that you've got every right to keep hoping.

I started running as if I knew what I'd see when I rounded our corner.

Phil Hargrove, monster white cast and all, standing there ringing our doorbell.

"Phil! How did you know where I live?"

"Oh, I can find my way around a little, even without your help."

"You came to sell me a magazine or something?"

"How about a beat-up, but basically-in-good-condition friend? Who's not going steady anymore?" With a smile that lit up the pink stucco front of our house, he lunged down the steps toward me — stumbled, and fell into my arms.

About the Author

LAUREL TRIVELPIECE, an avid hiker, was once lost herself in the Sierra. She has written three other young adult novels and an adult novel of suspense, as well as short stories, poems, and plays.

Ms. Trivelpiece graduated from the University of California at Berkeley and now lives with her husband in Corte Madera, California, on the slope of "humongous" Mount Tamalpais.

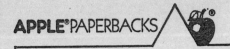